ANN CEDEÑO

Please Don't Repeat This

Print ISBN: 978-1-66785-355-0

eBook ISBN: 978-1-66785-356-7

CHAPTER ONE:

Sylvia Pearlman

I AM CONTENT AS I ENTER THE STAR OF DAVID Funeral Chapel after giving Sylvia Pearlman a manicure only days before. Her nails will be eternally beautiful.

The casket is closed. No one else will know Sylvia has on the latest pink shade from OPI's fall collection, but I do. The service is about to start, so I stop at the first empty seat I can find in the last row.

After working in the same area of South Florida for years and befriending countless women in the salon, paying my respects is the least I can do when they or their loved ones pass. Some services are more painful to sit through—unexpected deaths of the young, for example—but Sylvia lived a long, healthy life, and for that, I am thankful so I could have the chance to know her. I've learned so much from my clients that I may never have gained an understanding of otherwise.

The lights are dim, and the only sounds are hushed whispers. I sit wrapped in plush velvet under the cool breeze of the vent above me and recognize the backs of several mourners' heads. As large as my clientele is, it always surprises me to see how the various women know each other or somehow connect.

The daughter of the deceased, Kate, naturally is in the front row next to her husband and children. Her head is down, and she dabs her eyes with a tissue. She is also my client and the other reason I am here. She never has her nails done with any other girl in the salon, but our monogamous relationship would abruptly sever if I were to miss her mother's funeral.

Kate is a scorekeeper. There was the usual outpouring of generosity when her mother passed, and a list of who delivered what to her door that later she would access as a reference when they lose someone. Those who sent a platter will get a platter, and the card-givers a card.

The rabbi begins by listing Sylvia's trials and tribulations from her childhood or the lean years and then moves on to the better part of her life, which was anything but, and I only have one thought, This man has never met her. You can always tell when a stranger performs the service. Their delivery is awkward, and they keep looking at the family for reassurance. Too bad he isn't privy to the stories she told me over the years. They are far more entertaining.

When Sylvia's second husband was still alive, they traveled extensively. After a few years of doing her manicures, she finally confessed the vacations every summer were for swingers only.

"Doesn't your husband get jealous of the other men?" I asked.

"A little."

"Does it cause problems?"

"He's too busy to think about what I'm doing," she laughed.

"Do you ever regret it?"

"Not at all. It's very freeing. And once we get home, we never discuss what happened again."

No one else knew what the trips entailed and I'm honored she trusted me with her secrets over her daughter.

I met Sylvia long past her prime, and all I can say is she must have been a stunning woman in her youth. A beautiful woman never loses her sparkle even after skin sags and flaws become more pronounced.

Evolving with age and never losing one's sex appeal is not cheap. Being penniless in youth is fine, but it costs a fortune to keep up beauty for the long term. A diamond necklace can camouflage a wrinkly chest, and arthritic hands are not the focus, dripping in designer jewels.

Even without gaining a pound, no woman can avoid the natural shifting of body parts. Each season when Sylvia's salesgirl from Saks Fifth Avenue called to let her know the latest items had arrived, she added a few pieces to her collection, keeping her look conservative yet current. Expensive clothing worn the right way can hide any flaws. Sylvia's motto was, "When something doesn't look good anymore, cover it up!"

Sylvia's daughter, Kate, is not light-hearted like her mother. Her husband is a successful businessman; they have a son she hardly mentions and a daughter who behaves like a princess. She earned a degree in creative writing that she never did anything with, instead choosing the role of a stay-at-home mom who never stays at home.

In the salon, Kate approaches my desk like a dark cloud. The client in the chair has to stop talking mid-sentence when she stands there staring, and after an uncomfortable silence, she asks the dreaded question, "Are you running on time?"

"Have a seat. I won't be long," I say, but I can feel her stare burning the back of my head while I rush to finish.

No one knows what is happening in someone else's life. Kate plods through the salon like a woman who has it all, but her daughter, Nicole, has given her trouble as far back as I can remember. At ten, she came to my station with an expensive shampoo and conditioner in her hands, expecting her mother to buy it. When Kate said, "No, you don't need it," Nicole reached up and pulled her hair from behind. I saw Kate's head snap back in my peripheral vision as I was polishing, but she never flinched, and neither of us acknowledged the assault.

During spring break in high school, Nicole called her mother during another appointment. I could only hear one side of the conversation, and I never looked up—my attempt at giving her privacy.

Kate's diamond solitaire shone like a tiny light bulb under my task lamp. "No, you may not drive to the beach with friends," she said, and I felt her fingers stiffen.

"I don't care if everyone else is allowed."

Some people are not self-aware enough on their phones. Clients were glaring.

"No. You may not, and that's final. Please don't ask me again. Maybe your friends' parents don't care about them, but I care about you. I said no! Please stop asking me." And with that, seemingly involuntary, her hand smacked the top of my desk, and my heart jumped. I picked up my pace, and she continued, "I told you no. I'm having my nails done, and I'm supposed to be relaxing! Enough already."

Then I watched the retreat. Kate sat silent for a moment while Nicole pled her case. "I'm the worst parent? How can you say that?" And her tone shifted, "What time are they coming back? You better use sunscreen and be home for dinner."

Nicole always won. Like when she insisted on sharing a luxury apartment the first year of college with a friend instead of staying in the dorm rooms on campus. Moving day came, and while the mother/daughter duo shopped for last-minute items and traveled by plane, Kate's handyman made the five-hour drive in Nicole's car and began building and setting up the IKEA furniture before they arrived. He also hung blackout shades, added shelves to the closet to accommodate Nicole's excess clothing and shoes, and unpacked the car.

Weeks passed, and Kate still seemed wrapped up in Nicole's every move, texting and calling her all day long, so when an invitation came for a charity luncheon I encouraged her to go.

She wore an Alice + Olivia dress for the occasion and searched for a genuine friend to talk to among the women in her social circle. The other ladies, dressed equally unthrifty, seemed like they were having the time of their lives now that their children were out of the house, and she imagined she was the only one who had issues. Her phone lit up with Nicole's picture, and she was almost thankful for the interruption, tired of participating in the charade.

She then excused herself and took the call outside.

"Mom, I need you to Venmo Ashley. I'm moving to her apartment. I cannot live with Jessica anymore."

"What?"

"Jessica is psycho. Last night, she got drunk and slept with a guy she knows I like! If you don't send the money to Ashley right now, she will give the room to someone else."

"Hang on a second. I have a lease on your apartment. If you leave it, I still have to pay the rent."

The heat and humidity felt like an oven. Sweat trickled down her back as Nicole's voice became more threatening.

"I'm never going back there! I will quit school!"

"I can't talk to you right now. I'm at a luncheon."

"You don't have time to talk to your daughter? Real nice, Mom."

Kate, full-on sweating at this point, said, "I deserve time to myself. I will call you back later."

"I can't believe you." Nicole's voice cracked. My friends all say that their moms would let them move. What is your problem?"

"Fine, text me the amount," Kate said. Anything to hang up the phone and get back to the air-conditioning.

We later discussed how she would be paying rent on both apartments.

"I had no choice. What was I supposed to do?" Kate asked, and I stayed quiet, hoping she might realize how this sounds, spoken aloud, but she did not.

Without her children at home, this mom wasn't sure what her purpose was anymore. She spent evenings shopping while her husband conducted business out of town. Salespeople recognized her as a regular customer and tracked her every move inside the stores. "How are you? May I help you find something today?" They chirped incessantly, and "Just looking" was her usual reply, always looking for something to fill the void inside. Then, high on the thrill of the purchases, she had dinner at one of the fancy restaurants in the plaza, and only there was she confident enough to dine alone, along with the other shoppers.

Her Louis Vuitton Epi leather purse and the shopping bags sat on the chair next to her like a familiar friend. The waiters brushed crumbs from the white tablecloth and refilled her drink in the candle-lit atmosphere. Nothing was good enough, though. She was forever sending back her entrée.

One afternoon, her husband came home dizzy and suffering from chest pain. An echocardiogram showed a blockage, and his cardiologist admitted him to the hospital for open-heart surgery.

While nurses prepped him, Kate had a manicure, not wanting to throw off her standing appointment.

I could smell her perfume before she came into view.

"Are you going to be late?" Kate asked, as usual, even after her call to see if I was on time.

"Almost finished."

"Good because I need to go to Bloomingdale's."

"Today?"

"I have to. I have a rewards coupon, and it expires tomorrow."

That afternoon, Sylvia arrived at the hospital to be with her daughter during the surgery. Kate had already finished her nail appointment, been to the mall, and was comfortably seated in the waiting area.

"Are you coming to my house for Thanksgiving?" Kate asked.

"You're cooking?"

"Catering."

"What should I bring?"

"Nothing, Mom, just yourself."

The headcount topped off at 17, and their home lent itself to entertaining a party of this size, with a massive island in the kitchen covered in trays of various aged cheese and meats, dried fruit, and nuts. Bottles of wine were ready to be uncorked, and the candles were ready to light, but the holiday would magnify the family's shortcomings. It was easy for Kate to avoid past resentments with her mother most days having only brief phone conversations. But seeing her was a reminder.

Was it fair to assume that Sylvia would constantly babysit when the children were small because she lived in the same town? She had earned her station in life and chose to fill her social calendar while still young enough to enjoy herself. She loved her grandchildren from afar, but didn't interfere in their raising.

For this reason, the children were not particularly close to their grandmother. You get what you give.

Kate stomped into the kitchen where her husband, still not one hundred percent, was seated at the table. "The food was supposed to be here at two fifteen," she said.

He rolled his eyes, knowing a scene was about to unfold. His wife always reacted the same.

"Get the owner, please," she screeched into the phone.

"He's busy at the moment. Can I help you?"

"Tell him it's Kate. His daughter, Becky, is one of my closest friends."

The owner stopped what he was doing and got on the phone.

"We are running a little late, dear, with all the holiday orders, but the driver should be there soon."

"I have guests arriving at four."

"Relax, my darling. I assure you the driver is on his way."

She couldn't relax and called the restaurant to complain again, but no one answered.

"Go take a shower, Kate," her husband said. The housekeeper was there, too, perfectly capable of receiving the order.

"I will not take a shower until the food arrives! What if my order is wrong?"

Finally, the driver pulled in at three-thirty, where Kate met him in the driveway. "My guests will be here any moment. I hope you are happy; you have succeeded in ruining my holiday."

"I'm sorry, ma'am."

It was a warm day, warmer than usual in November, and the trays appeared slimy from condensation. She had no choice but to accept the platters and then spend another twenty minutes calling the restaurant to demand a partial refund. At the same time, the housekeeper transferred the food into serving platters.

With barely enough time to get dressed before the first guest rang the doorbell, Kate worked herself into a hot flash. As she emerged from her bedroom, her Ted Baker skirt was sticking to her legs.

Although the house had ambiance, the table sparkling with crystal, and the smell of the traditional Thanksgiving meal in the air, the hostess was not gracious to her guests. Nothing is worse than being at someone's house when it's clear they regret having anyone over.

Her mother encouraged her, raving about the food, but Kate never even tasted it, convinced it was spoilt. Nicole jumped up to leave as the housekeeper cleared the table and refilled the glasses. Sylvia turned to her granddaughter and gave her a stern look.

"We haven't had dessert yet."

"Grandma, my friends are waiting for me."

And after all the expense and aggravation, the day left Kate feeling empty. The beautiful home was only an illusion, not an indication of the couple's happiness.

When Sylvia died, Kate, in charge of the arrangements, found Nicole lounging in her bedroom, and with teary eyes, she asked, "Can you please come to the funeral home with me? I need to bring the outfit we are burying Grandma in, and I don't want to go alone."

"Not happening," was her daughter's response.

Kate suddenly missed her mother, or the comfort of knowing she was there unconditionally. The love only a mother provides. If only she had spent more time with her before it was too late. There is free time now to do the things she loves, but ironically she has forgotten what those things are. A friend asks what music she likes, and she admits she doesn't even have a playlist, always borrowing her husband's when the rare time comes that she listens.

During her mother's service, Kate considers writing again. She remembers a notebook of poetry she started during college that is probably still in the attic. The rabbi stops speaking, and we all stand to leave. Again, there are whispers. This time, one sounds familiar. A friend of Sylvia's says what a lovely service it was, but that's never where it stays. With a curdled look, the stocky woman behind her says, "But did you see her daughter? She doesn't seem very sad."

On my way out, I search for Kate. She is standing near the exit of the dark lobby alongside her family. I signed the guest book on the way in, but I need to show my face after the service. I don't want her to think I left early. There is a line of people waiting to offer condolences. Finally, it is my turn.

"I'm so sorry for your loss," I say.

"Thank you for coming, Annie," she says. Then I rush to my car. I need to get back to the salon for my one fifteen appointment.

CHAPTER TWO:
Isabel Edelstein

ISABEL THROWS A LOCK OF LONG BLONDE HAIR OVER her shoulder at one twenty-five and adjusts herself in the chair. Her tight, round belly makes it difficult to get close to the table.

"I'm having a C-section next week. Can you come over to do my nails when I get home?"

"Why a C-section?" I ask as I remove her polish.

"My pelvic bones are small, and my doctor is afraid I might have trouble delivering, but more than that, he prefers his patients not wake him when they go into labor in the middle of the night."

"I guess it's better for you, too, knowing when it will happen."

"Yes, and they let me choose the birthdate. 2-15-2015."

"That's hard to forget," I say. It doesn't surprise me that Isabel has a say in the day her baby will be born. She has a way of orchestrating everything.

"Right? And I should be ready for you to come over to do my nails on the 27th."

Isabel and I have become friendly; otherwise, I would not say yes to the favor.

Doing nails in someone's house is never an ideal situation. The poor lighting, the phone ringing, and other distractions make it difficult, and I miss out on several appointments in the salon. But what I lose with one client, I make up with another, and I know Isabel is not the type to expect me to do her nails at home without properly compensating me.

I ascend the long driveway to the double front doors, and Richard, her husband, lets me in. He is tall and slim and curiously only attractive if you know he is a doctor.

The floors in the entrance are light wood, and there is sparse modern furniture throughout.

"Your home is beautiful," I say.

"Thank you, but I can't take credit. It was all Isabel." His wife has a flair for design and is obsessed with every detail, but she didn't do everything. He at least paid for it.

Immediately to the left through a small vestibule is the primary bedroom, where the new mom is propped up in the oversized king bed holding her baby.

"Thank you so much for coming," Isabel says.

"My pleasure. I wanted to meet Mia anyway."

"Well, here she is. Hopefully, she will sleep for a little while."

I glimpse a flawless little face with rosebud lips that gets passed to her husband, who takes away the sleeping baby. I spread out my supplies on a table that is too low and sit down on a chair provided that is too high and have to hunch over to do the manicure in this awkward position. A lamp behind me makes matters worse, casting a shadow over the nails. I finish quickly and straighten up, and Isabel looks down at her polish, seemingly pleased.

"Come, let me show you the nursery," she says with her hands up, waving her arms back and forth in stiff tiny strokes like a bird in mid-flight.

I'm surprised how far away the baby's room is from hers. They will have to use a monitor to hear her cries and then trudge the length of a football field to get to her.

The room is white and simple, with a pink plush area rug. The crib is Lucite, and a faint scent of paint is in the air. Isabel is ambling, her hand on her stomach.

"It's a good thing I had a C-section. Mia's cord was around her neck."

"I'm so glad you are both okay."

"Me too."

After a moment, we travel down another corridor to the kitchen, where a giant three-wick candle burns in the otherwise dark space. Richard is watching a movie on the sofa nearby, and Mia is still asleep next to him. He sees us and hands me a hundred-dollar bill.

"Thank you," I say, and Isabel looks at me pleadingly.

"Do you have to leave?" In this rare moment off from her new role as a mother, she wants me to hang out with her. "I can open a bottle of champagne," she says and succeeds in enticing me to stay a little longer.

"You can drink?"

"Sure. I'm not breastfeeding."

The sun lowers over their rectangular swimming pool as we sit on the loveseat, sipping champagne out of paper-thin crystal flutes. On the oriental rug beneath our feet are a pair of Gucci sandals that Isabel absently discarded. I notice the stitching on the tiny straps and admire the detail, and I'm impressed by the exemplary life of the couple who live here.

She is back in the salon for her next appointment, showing off the baby with the same blonde hair and brown eyes as she does. The sight of them together, the baby a soft blur wrapped in chenille blankets and pink bows and the mother beaming with pride, is a vision to envy.

"You look great," I tell her.

"I still need to lose fifteen pounds, so no more fast food."

During her pregnancy, Isabel craved Taco Bell and didn't think about what havoc the meat-filled tortillas were doing to her body, and only now regrets the indulgence.

"I hired a personal trainer at the gym," she says.

"Who will watch the baby?"

"Richard will have to do it on his mornings off from seeing patients. We are raising this baby 50/50. I'm not doing all the work."

Instead of playing golf like he always had, her husband agrees to change diapers and feed the baby while his wife works out with a trainer. And in the evenings, she hands over the baby the moment he walks in the door, even if it is only to put away her impeccably folded laundry.

Mia's dresser contains dozens of onesies, socks, and matching blankets itemized the same way as the high-end baby stores that carry them. And likewise, every closet and pantry in the house has the same type of multiple inventories. Isabel squirrels her things to suggest she didn't always have money and fears losing it. But she masters the role of wife and mother quickly, and I watch her walk to the shampoo bowl a year later, her stomach completely flat, maybe even slightly concave in her expensive yoga pants. She wasn't born a natural beauty, but she puts herself together well, camouflaging any imperfections.

After her hair appointment, she sits at my desk for her mani-cure, and the previous client, still drying her nails, listens to Isabel talk about herself; she puts on quite a show.

"Richard can't get enough of me since I lost weight. He says he likes having his tiny wife back," she brags. And I can't help encouraging her. "You are fortunate," I say.

"I thought he would be upset when the credit card state-ment came in this month, but I was wearing a pair of short shorts while he read over the bill, and he never said a word when he saw the total."

The other client, a sour-faced woman, acted like she wasn't listening, but it was too hard not to.

"Last night was date night at a restaurant near the beach," Isabel continued.

"Really, where?" I ask.

"Valentino's. The restaurant was full, but I insisted I made an online reservation, and the hostess found us a table."

"How was the food?" the client spoke up, intrigued.

"We shared a salad and a shrimp entrée. I told Richard I wouldn't go if he planned on ordering a ton of food."

"And your husband was okay with that?"

"Of course."

"Her husband is the sweetest," I chime in, and the client practically rolls her eyes and walks away. Either Richard likes being told what to do, or it is just easier for him in the long run, but he even drives Mia each day when she starts preschool so that his wife can get ready for her daily workout at the gym in peace.

Isabel rises early one misty fall morning and dresses before waking the baby. Richard waits in the car with his double shot of espresso until his wife straps Mia into her seat and kisses her goodbye. Then they drive away, and Isabel makes the beds and straightens up until everything is in place. Before leaving the house, she takes one last admiring glance at her silhouette in the mirror and sprays herself with her favorite perfume.

On the way to the gym, she stops for a car wash. A man dressed for the office and a dowdy housewife also wait for the complimentary service in the plush lounge of the Mercedes dealership.

Isabel ignores the customers as if they don't exist and chooses a coffee with hazelnut-flavored cream, avoiding the sugar and the fresh fruit-filled pastries on the counter bar. Within minutes, the unsavory salesman who originally sold them the SUV walks over. "Wow, you look great."

"Thanks," she says and turns away. Something in her mannerisms suggests she's available, and it attracts men like flies.

It's subtle the way she flirts now. No more hair pulled up in a ponytail and a face with no makeup, and it's not her outfit, but the way the pants cling and the jacket opens below her bra line that begs attention. She stands twirling her hair between sets at the gym, knowing she's driving the younger guys crazy. It becomes a challenge to see which one she will talk to first, and Steven, a stocky guy with dark hair, is the winner.

He sees her on the track, walks behind her, and then steps inside her scent. The clean powdery notes of her expensive perfume indicate she is a step up from the girls he has been with thus far.

"Do you run?" he asks.

"I walk."

"Mind if I join you?"

"Sure."

Isabel looks tiny next to Steven. His skin glistens and stretches over the muscles on his arms.

"Where do you work? I always see you here in the morning."

"I'm a firefighter."

She noticed his truck in the parking lot and assumed his job was something manly. "You must have a lot of time off."

"I do, but I'm working tonight. Why don't you come to see me at the fire station?"

"I have dinner plans with girlfriends."

"Text me when you finish," Steven says. He puts his hand out, and Isabel swipes open her phone. The photo of Mia vanishes, and Steven enters his number.

"What should I name myself so your husband won't see?" He is staring at her diamond eternity band.

"He doesn't look at my phone," Isabel says. "What about you? Are you married?"

"No."

"Dating?"

"Something like that."

"Living together?"

"For now," and his answer implies that the relationship is not serious. The firefighter quickly walks off at the next exit on the track, leaving her to finish the workout by herself.

From the car, she calls Richard. "Make sure you are home on time tonight; I need you to watch Mia."

He hesitates for a second, and then Isabel is all over him. "I have a birthday dinner with the girls," she says, annoyed.

"Oh, yes, I remember. I will be home by seven."

Isabel is in the garage, all set to leave when her husband gets home. She has on a pair of slim jeans and a halter top, and the heels of her shoes make her legs look even longer than they are. Richard moves toward her, but by the time he reaches her vehicle, she's already behind the wheel.

"Mia is sleeping," she instructs. He leans in and her peppermint mouthwash mixes with the new car smell. "And there is leftover Chinese in the refrigerator."

"I had a late lunch. I'm going to grab a beer and watch the game."

"I need to go, I don't want to be late for the girls."

Girls' dinners have always bored Isabel. The thought of sitting through one tonight with Steven only blocks away, waiting to see her, is too much, and she picks up her phone.

"Siri, call Dana." She pictures her closest friend, probably at the restaurant beforehand, scoping out the best seat at the table.

"I can't make it. Something came up. You guys have fun without me," Isabel says. The soft music and silverware rattling in the background confirm her suspicion. Dana refuses to sit at the end of the table where she can't participate in every conversation.

"Is everything all right?"

"Fine, I will explain later."

Isabel makes a U-turn at the next intersection toward the fire station.

Her palms feel clammy at the sight of Steven next to the gigantic red engine. She has no qualms about being married and seen by the other firefighters dressed in their gear. They stop talking and stare when Isabel walks toward the building.

"You have good timing. We got back a few minutes ago," Steven says.

"What happened?"

"A car accident."

"Is everyone all right?"

"We transported two people to the hospital, but the injuries are minor."

"That's good."

He smiles and looks her up and down, his eyes landing on the shiny gold Rolex she's wearing. "Did you dress up for me?"

"I guess so since I never made it to the restaurant."

The other guys try to be nonchalant as Steven parades her past them like a first-place prize.

"I wasn't expecting you this early."

"I didn't feel like sitting there all night."

"What did you tell your friends?"

"Nothing, they wouldn't understand. Half of them are pregnant, the rest in full mommy mode," she says. Steven's eyes widen. "I like mommy mode. I think it's sexy. Come on, let's go inside."

Something that smells like onions are cooking on the stove when the heavy door cracks open. Another fireman in a plain white t-shirt at the table gives his co-worker a nod of approval. In her stilettos, Isabel prances across the dingy floor to keep up with Steven, who holds her hand, dragging her out a rear exit.

He leans against the door to close it behind them and pulls her close. The night is dark, but the stars are bright in the sky.

"I'm crazy about you," he says. "If I could leave right now, I would take you somewhere and rape you."

She laughs. There is no place to go.

Isabel's phone vibrates, and Mia's photo pops up on the screen when she denies the call. Steven holds her hand steady to see it.

"Is that your baby?"

"Yes."

"How old is she?"

"Thirty-eight months." Some new moms count every month. He looks confused, "She's three years old then?"

"Yes."

"And is that your husband calling you?"

"No, it's my friend Dana."

Dana owns a condo on the beach, and it occurs to Isabel it is the perfect place to take Steven.

"I might know somewhere we can go tomorrow," she says, and Steven pulls her close, kissing the spot on her neck just under her earlobe.

After ten, Isabel calls her friend back; by then, Dana is already home.

The phone rings several times until finally, she picks up.

"Hey, Isabel."

"Hey, if your husband asks, please don't mention that I didn't go to dinner tonight."

"Okay, but I don't think he'll ask. Why? What's going on with you?"

"I can't say right now, but I wondered, is the condo going to be empty tomorrow?"

"Yes. The renters left last week. Do you want to meet at the beach club?"

"I was hoping to get away by myself, a little alone time."

"Should I be worried about you, Isabel?"

"Not at all. Just trying to work some things out."

"The key is at the front desk. I have to go. The baby is crying."

I notice an air of mischief when Isabel comes in weeks later for her next nail appointment, but I don't have to wonder what it is. I can tell she's been holding this secret, unable to tell anyone else, and once she starts, the words pour out like running water.

"You met him at the gym?"

"Yes. We have been flirting for a while."

She scrolls through her phone and shows me a photo of a tanned, muscular guy—the total opposite of her husband.

"Don't cheat, Isabel. I have seen many girls with far less than you have, throw away their husbands and then regret it."

"But isn't he cute?" she asks, and I feel like I'm back in middle school.

"What does he do for a living?"

"He's a firefighter."

"I can't see you with a firefighter."

"Why not?"

"Because you are married to a doctor. And you have a daughter with him." And honestly, I can't picture Isabel walking through the fire station in her expensive clothing.

"He's also a paramedic. I'm sure he makes money."

"Not close to what you have now."

"I will get a settlement from Richard."

"How long will that last?"

"He has to give me half of everything."

My face tells her it's not enough.

"And I think Steven has family money, too," she adds.

But I know the firefighter isn't looking for anything serious by how she describes him.

"Steven watches me the entire time I'm with the trainer, but he leaves the gym right before my session ends."

"Only a player behaves like that."

"No, he's not a player."

"Does he have a girlfriend?"

"Yes, but she's not his type at all. She's a school teacher," she says, making a face.

I feel for Isabel. Listening to the story is better than any soap opera, but why risk all she has? It is only a fluke that she got to this station in life. Richard's mother was against the marriage, but Isabel won that battle. She is used to getting what she wants and is determined, although this guy, Steven, makes no effort. Sure he can't resist the steamy X-rated sex in his truck parked behind the fire station, and he accepts the elaborate meals Isabel brings him almost daily. Still, none of it is his idea, and even when she plans something as involved as acquiring the condo for the day, he lazily shows up, going to the gym first.

It must sting, sitting alone in the condo with the breathtaking view waiting for a guy you have to persuade to come with a tray of food wilting and a bottle of expensive champagne slowly losing its frost. But when he finally arrives and wordlessly carries her to the bedroom, she forgives him.

"Are you hungry?" Isabel asks afterward.

"Starving."

Isabel pops the cork and pours some champagne for Steven.

"Maybe I can bring Mia here next time so you can meet her."

"Whoa. I'm not ready for kids."

"Well, get ready. I will have Mia half the time after my divorce."

Isabel feeds Steven fresh sushi from wooden chopsticks and doesn't notice the red flag.

"Don't get divorced for me," he says, "I'm not jumping from one relationship into another."

But Isabel doesn't believe him.

The next day Dana meets her to pick up the key.

"I have to tell you something."

"What is it?"

"I have been lying to Richard and saying I'm with you."

"What?"

"I met someone at the gym, a firefighter; his body is incredible," she says dreamily.

"Are you crazy? What if Richard finds out? Wait, is that why you wanted the condo?"

"We didn't have anywhere else to go. Steven lives with his girlfriend, but not for much longer," Isabel giggles.

"Have you lost your mind, or are you trying to ruin your life?"

"I'm in love, Dana. I found an apartment only a few blocks from the fire station, and I've already told Richard."

"What did you say?"

"That I'm not happy."

"And?"

"And he says he wants custody of Mia."

"Are you staying in the house?"

"I don't want the house."

"Did the firefighter say he would marry you?"

"I'm sure he will once I'm single."

But Steven is in a different headspace, frequently sneaking out of the gym without saying goodbye. One morning, she catches him and runs up to the passenger side of his truck. He reluctantly unlocks the door.

"Why didn't you say goodbye?"

"I didn't see you."

"Do you want to get a smoothie?"

"I guess," he says.

The seat barely moves as the weight of her tiny frame lands in the center. When the truck pulls away, she turns to face her boyfriend. The air shifts from carefree to something else entirely, and there is a heaviness in it, causing her to feel insecure. Still, she brushes it off and checks her jacket pocket to ensure she has enough money for the drinks because paying for Steven's things in the past only set precedence, and now he doesn't ever offer.

They drive around sipping the overpriced green organic drinks and pass Isabel's development.

"This is my neighborhood."

"The houses look huge."

"They are. I want something smaller next time."

He ignores the prompt to talk about a future together and speaks as if his situation isn't changing.

"I've been looking for a house, but I'm still paying my student loans. I owe another thirty thousand, and then I can apply for a mortgage."

"Where is your place? Can we drive by it?"

"I'm in the townhouses near the fire station," he says. Given the flashy truck he drives, Isabel knows it will be easy to find.

Instead of getting out when they arrive back at her SUV, she lingers inside the truck, hoping he will suggest they see each other again soon, but he looks restless. The longer she hesitates, the more uncomfortable it becomes.

Steven is even less friendly when she shows up unannounced at the fire station the next time.

"I brought the sushi you like."

"You didn't have to do that."

"I wanted to."

"We need to cool things off for a while. Beth knows something's up." Hearing her name for the first time feels like a punch in the stomach.

"Why? What happened?" Isabel asks.

"She found your lip gloss in my truck."

"What did she say?" Isabel pictures the shiny pink tube of Dior between the seats where she placed it, hoping to break them up. Steven is vague with his answer, "She's pissed." He goes back inside, with the bag containing the sushi.

Isabel drives back home, taking her frustration out on Richard. He is still trying to salvage the marriage two weeks before she moves out.

"I thought you would be a while," he says. "I'm about to start a movie if you want to watch it with me."

"Watching a movie with you is the last thing I want to do right now. I'm going to bed." Intimacy has ended. She sleeps early every night and propels herself out of bed in the morning if Richard tries to touch her.

Besides an enormous check and her personal belongings, she takes the best modern furniture pieces from the house. Each appears much more significant in the small space of the apartment and doesn't make sense, like placing rare diamonds in a gold-plated bracelet.

She expects Steven to come running back now that they have a place to be alone. The pantry has his favorite snacks, and there is a garage for him to park his truck so it won't be seen, but he continues to avoid her.

Finally, she has an idea. And sends a text.

I want to pay off your student loan.

It works. Steven can't resist the offer. The following day after his shift, he comes over to get the money, and the affair is back on.

Who wouldn't want someone on the side attending to every whim? For months, they play house together in the apartment.

Things may have gone on indefinitely, but he immediately falls asleep on Isabel's bed one morning after a busy night at work. She massages lotion on his chest, and he smiles with his eyes closed and dozes off again. Isabel grabs her razor and shaves his entire front, wiping the hair off the razor as she goes with a tissue.

"What have you done?" he says when he sees himself in the mirror.

"What's the worst thing that happens? Beth gets mad and leaves you?"

When Isabel comes in to have her nails done the next time, I can tell she has been crying.

"What's wrong?"

"Nothing."

"Is it Steven?"

"Yes. I drove past the townhouse last night, and I could see them sitting on the couch together through the front window," she says.

"Isn't that stalking?"

"He promised he was going to break up with her."

"Maybe he will."

"I think she might break up with him."

"Why?"

"I wrote her a letter."

"What kind of letter?"

"I told her that Steven is cheating on her and included our text messages with the time stamp as proof. I'm putting it on her windshield when I leave here."

"Don't, Isabel. Once you do it, you can never undo it."

"I know, and I don't care. I'm also sending a copy to the principal at the school where she works, just in case someone else finds the one on her car before she does."

"No one likes a fatal attraction. You will ruin your chances."

"I refuse to let Steven pretend I don't exist."

Then Julie walks up. "Isabel, I was looking for you. Aren't you supposed to have a blow-dry with me today?"

"Yes, sorry I was late."

"Go get shampooed, and I can do it here."

Isabel walks away, and Julie asks, "What's wrong with her?"

"She's upset over her boyfriend."

"I thought she's married to a doctor."

"She was."

Isabel has the nerve to show up at the fire station two weeks after the letters went out. There has been no contact from Steven and she doesn't see his truck in the parking lot. One of the firefighters catches her snooping and walks up to her SUV.

"Is Steven working tonight?"

"He's in Vegas."

"What's he doing there?"

"Getting married."

"What?"

"He had no choice after the letter you sent. Beth was going to leave him."

"It proves he cheated on her with me."

"I know, but he told her you were some psycho who follows him around the gym."

"He's a liar."

"People believe what they want," he says.

A year later, Isabel re-emerges as an expert at online dating with the same enthusiasm she always had.

"I met a guy."

"I'm so happy for you."

"He's a pilot."

"Nice."

"How long have you been together?"

"Not long, but I can tell he wants a future with me."

"I'm sure."

I couldn't help thinking she was looking for something she already had once before.

"What's going on with Richard? Do you ever see him?"

"I saw him at Mia's school last week. Did I tell you he's getting remarried?"

"No, you didn't mention it."

"He's so predictable. Everyone says his fiancée looks exactly like me."

"Do you think you should have stayed with him?"

"No way," she says, as if I am the crazy one.

If she admits leaving her husband was a mistake, it would mean she destroyed her own life, something that is difficult to accept.

CHAPTER THREE:

Linsey Jacobs

LINSEY HAS ON A CAMEL LEATHER MINI SKIRT, A BONE cashmere sweater, and a pair of matching Louboutins at the salon for her nail appointment. The look is over-the-top for daytime, especially with her diamond-encrusted Rolex, but she pulls it off.

Some clients are a pleasure and a wealth of knowledge I hope to absorb during our conversations. Over the years, we have become close, celebrating our accomplishments and mourning our losses. They laugh easily, wait patiently, and are never a bother.

Linsey is not that client.

The airs she puts on are unwarranted, but that's often the way in South Florida, where the line between rich and poor is blurred. She's originally from Lansing, Michigan, and I wonder what makes her such a princess.

As a teen, Linsey spent a lot of time with the family of her best friend, Kristen Harrison. Kristen's father is a prominent orthodontist, who aligned the bites of over half of their friends. And Mrs. Harrison, originally from Chicago, is a woman of class and means. She took the girls with her on one of her shopping trips to The Windy City, unknowingly introducing Linsey to specialty designer apparel.

The high-end department store had clothing made of colorful, delicate fabrics, and while Mrs. Harrison shopped, the girls snuck the most expensive dresses they could find into a fitting room. Kristen chose an orange knit, and Linsey tried on a green silk slip number. Looking at themselves in the mirror, they started laughing and couldn't stop.

The designer gowns swam on their prepubescent bodies. They both had shoulder-length bobs. Kristen's blonde and wild like a bad perm, and Linsey's dark and straight, but Kristen had her shirt over her head, pretending it was long hair.

Mrs. Harrison heard the muffled giggles and called out to them.

"I hope you girls are behaving yourselves!"

"We are!"

"Do not embarrass me."

"We won't!"

When she returned home, Linsey looked around her house as if for the first time. Why did her mother choose such ordinary things?

"Your father is not a professional like Kristen's," her mother explained, with her father sitting right there watching the news.

Kristen is unaware of the difference, having always had the best, and is fortunate enough to take her privileged upbringing for granted. Fancy weekend dinners, ski trips, and spring break in sunny Florida are the norm for her, and she was away on vacation the summer before their senior year of high school when Linsey got into trouble.

Linsey worked that summer as a camp counselor, and after hours of arts and crafts, tetherball, and boating on the lake, she was sunburned, mosquito-bitten, and exhausted by the ten fourth-graders in her charge. When the kids finally went home for the day, the teens who worked there got together to swim on the far side of the same lake, where they drank beer until dark.

The beer-drinking parties lead to unprotected sex, and for Linsey, it had more to do with getting through the long summer days without her best friend than love. She was naive enough to believe the pull-out method would prevent pregnancy but, of course, it does not, and two weeks before school started, Linsey had to have an abortion. In the back of her mind, this was always her safety net. Rumors went around that two girls at school had abortions already, and they seemed fine.

The boy paid half for the procedure, but did not accompany her to the appointment or call her again. And while millions of girls have gone through the same scenario, it affects each one differently.

Kristen enjoyed every moment of her senior year, but Linsey struggled with what happened.

"You have to snap out of it," Kristen said.

"I'm trying."

"You're fine. It's over, and we have to think about college now."

It was easy for Kristen. She had a 4.0 GPA and scored high on the SAT. Her hard work allowed her to choose where to study, but her dream was to attend the University of Miami.

"Why don't you come with me? You can stay with me at my apartment."

"I've never been to Miami."

"That's my point. You need to get away from here, and you will love it!"

The whole application process is foreign to Linsey, who never kept up her grades and didn't have parents who paved the way for her to go to college like Kristen's. She planned to work full-time after graduation and take a class or two at the community college. Why not do that in Miami?

The problem was Mrs. Harrison didn't see the benefit of the friendship anymore.

"It's not that I don't like Linsey. I'm just afraid having her there will be a distraction."

"Don't lie, Mom. You never wanted me to be friends with Linsey."

"Is she going to contribute to the rent on your apartment?"

"Really? You know she doesn't have any money."

"You will meet new friends in Miami, more like you. You'll see."

Kristen left after graduation and met an entire group of friends in Miami who are, just like her mother said, exactly like her. Still, she missed Linsey, whose friendship has always been like a security blanket.

"When are you coming to visit?"

"As soon as I get enough for a plane ticket."

"Why not drive?"

"Do you think my car will make it?"

"Just get here."

Linsey left under the guise of going to Detroit for the weekend with friends and arrived here in Miami after dark the following day. She passes out on Kristen's couch.

"Wake up. It's a beach day, and everyone is going," Kristen says, shaking her arm.

"I don't have a bathing suit."

"You can wear one of mine."

A best friend's closet is always more appealing than your own, and Kristen will happily swap a pair of designer jeans for one of Linsey's thrift store vintage finds any day of the week, no questions asked.

Before the beach, Kristen brings Linsey into the salon for a Mani/Pedi, and I notice they differ from the girls in South Florida. More wholesome. They both choose a soft shade of pink for their nails.

The students gather in a semicircle of towels and chairs on the sand. The beach is hot, but more than that, it's humid, which is not ideal for Kristen's hair. Water might do it some good.

"Let's take a swim," Linsey suggests.

White foam wraps their ankles and disappears as they wade past the seaweed into the ocean. They stand for a while with the waves crashing against them.

"Isn't the beach amazing?" Kristen asks.

"It is, but I think I need to eat something."

"Don't worry. We have pretzels and beer."

Drinking is something Linsey vows not to do since alcohol clouded her judgment once before. "I'll walk to the market and see what they have."

"Do you want me to come with you?"

"No, I'm good."

The small bottle of fresh-squeezed orange juice and a cheese pastry costs over ten dollars. Linsey hands the cashier who doesn't speak English a twenty, takes her change, and then walks along the adjoining strip of stores.

As pure as the ocean air is on the beach, one would think that fifty yards away, the sidewalk would not smell like something has died, but it does. Part of it is the dumpsters behind the restaurants containing bits of discarded seafood left to rot in the sun, and part is garbage left by the nightlife that beachgoers trample over.

The juice is cold and sweet. Linsey needs to call her mother and tell her she's in Miami, then find a job before her money runs out. But not today. Today she will reinvent herself. And the first thing she does is pull out her phone and take a selfie with the caption, Welcome to Miami Beach. #beachvibes.

She wanders in and out of the open shops along A1A that carry swimwear. No one is around to help, so she picks out a few floral print bikinis with matching cover-ups and brings them into a mirrored dressing room to try on.

The first one has a price tag of one hundred thirty-five dollars, but she can't leave it behind. It fits like a glove and accentuates the proportions of her body in a way no other suit ever has. Is this why women pay top dollar for designer clothing? The entire garment fits into the palm of her hand, and how easy would it be to fold it up and stuff it into her purse?

Her blood sugar level, elevated from the juice, gives her a rush, and her heartbeat pounds in her eardrums. If she is to do this, she has to act fast. The empty hanger fits underneath another, hidden from view, and remains on the hook as she walks out with the bikini in her bag unnoticed to rejoin the group.

A week later, she lands a job at a high-end boutique that offers an employee discount and has already blended seamlessly into Kristen's friend group who live in the apartment complex. They all assume Linsey's parents also fund her living expenses if they even think about it, primarily concerned with her willingness to party. She attends the get-togethers, but still never drinks.

Half the girls end up drunk nightly, falling all over themselves, and if you have ever been at a party sober while everyone else is not, you know how it can test your patience. But with her wits about her, she fools them all, posing for pictures but not

ANN CEDEÑO

partaking in the consumption of the cheap vodka and amber ale by emptying her cup in the nearest receptacle when no one is looking.

Do the parents of these kids know their hard-earned money goes into funding enough alcohol to give the entire university a hangover? Linsey thinks not.

She tires of the nonsense by winter break when the students leave for a month to spend the holidays with their families.

"Did you get a flight home?" Kristen asks.

"No, I was hoping I could stay here. I have to work."

"Of course, you can."

"What are your plans?"

"My parents planned a trip to Cabo."

"Nice."

"Won't you be scared here by yourself?"

"No, not at all."

And there is no reason to be afraid. That wasn't the problem.

It's easy to be an adult when everything goes right, but to a nineteen-year-old, any obstacle feels like a catastrophe. On the third day in Miami by herself, her car breaks down while returning to the boutique from picking up lunch.

Linsey exits her car in a skin-tight dress, a bag in one hand containing the takeout containers and a tray of fountain sodas in the other. The store is only blocks away, but her high heels make the walk impossible. At least it happens on a busy street, directly in front of a furniture store where a cute guy, probably in his late twenties, is standing out front.

His back is to her, facing a dining room table and chairs on display. He sees her approach in the reflection of the glass and turns around.

"Is that your car?"

"Yes. It just stopped, and I can't get it started."

"Can I give you a ride? You can't walk carrying all that food."

"Thank you, I appreciate it. I work just around the corner, and I might get fired if I'm late."

"Can I ask you something first?"

"Sure."

"What do you think of this table?"

"I'm not a fan."

He bursts out laughing. Linsey's honesty is so refreshing after everyone else yeses him to death.

"Why? Do you work here?" Linsey asks.

"I'm Charles. I own the store."

"I'm Linsey." She tries to recover, "If it's any consolation, I like the green sofa behind it."

"That's one of our best sellers."

He turns and points to his Tesla. "Here, let me help you."

She hands over the heavy bags and sits in the molded seat.

"Are you going to eat all of this?"

"It's mostly for my co-workers."

Charles looks at the sign on the front of the building when they arrive at the boutique, committing it to memory.

"Hey, what about the car?"

"I don't know. What should I do?"

"I have a friend who is a mechanic. He can look at it."

"That would be great."

"What about the keys?"

"They're still in it."

"Okay. I'll call you soon."

"Thank you so much."

The store's manager, Marie, watches them exchange numbers from the register.

"I see you met Charles," she says when Linsey comes in.

"He gave me a ride. My car broke down. Why, do you know him?"

"Everyone knows him."

"What do you mean?"

"He's a confirmed bachelor. Will probably never settle down."

Linsey is in the back room unpacking boxes later when she hears her phone ring. She runs to the front and grabs it. It's Charles.

"Hey, what time do you get off?" he asks.

"Around nine."

"Your car is ready."

"Really? How much do I owe?"

"Nothing. I told you it's my friend's shop."

"Thank you so much."

"Don't thank me, have dinner with me tonight. I know a late-night spot we can go on South Beach."

Marie disapproves. True, he is slightly older, but after months of drunk students hitting on her, Charles in his grown-up car with his grown-up Ferragamo shoes has some appeal. And maybe Marie is just jealous.

Girls. We make excuses for a guy's behavior before getting to know his true character, and even when it's obvious he's not worth our time, we still want to believe he is.

The evening is unlike anything Linsey has ever experienced. She tries sushi for the first time, then walks into a club next to Charles like arm candy. They end up at his condo in Fort Lauderdale and watch the sunrise. He serves her breakfast on the balcony.

"I don't want to leave, but I have an early meeting," he says reluctantly.

"Can you drop me at my apartment?"

"Why? You can take my car to work. I'll use my truck."

"That's not the problem. I can't wear the same dress to work again," Linsey says, pointing to herself.

Charles hands her a wad of cash. "Sleep here for a while, and then buy whatever you need."

When he leaves, she counts the money. It's more than her weekly paycheck; it feels like she won the lottery. And for Charles, a pretty young girl that is so easily impressed is a boost to his ego. They are the perfect match.

Every second she isn't working, Charles wants her at his condo, and what better way to spend her time than with him. On the weekends, he takes her out and gives her more money for shopping, and she finally knows how Mrs. Harrison must feel, being taken care of like this.

Kristen returns from Cabo and finds her apartment exactly how she left it; no one around has seen or heard from Linsey. She grabs her phone and opens the favorites page where Linsey's number is at the top.

"Where are you?" Kristen asks.

"I'm at Neiman Marcus in Bal Harbor. You should see the dresses I'm looking at right now. Can you FaceTime?"

"No. I just got out of the shower. Have you been with the furniture store guy this whole time?"

"Pretty much."

"You must like him."

"Love. I love him."

Kristen giggles. "I'm happy for you, then."

When Linsey finally Ubers over to Kristen's apartment to get her things, there isn't much to take. Mostly clothes and the car she hasn't driven since having it repaired.

With the last load in her arms, she fumbles with the trunk's lock before it finally pops open. How did she ever drive this thing that doesn't have a hands-free trunk? If she gets dirt from the bumper on her new bathing suit cover-up, she will lose it. With any luck, the weather will hold so she can sit by the pool to get some color before tonight's dinner reservation. Her white mini dress looks so much better with a tan, and she plans to get a photo with Charles to post on social media. She parks her car in the underground parking garage of the condo, on the other side of the several vehicles her boyfriend owns. All brand new. As she enters the residence with her clothing, the cleaning girl stops her.

"Miss, this receipt fell behind the nightstand. Maybe you need it?"

The receipt is for two dozen roses purchased the week before by Charles and delivered to a girl named Kim. There has to be some explanation.

"It was her birthday. I have always sent her flowers on her birthday," Charles says.

"I live with you now. You can't tell me you think sending roses to your ex-girlfriend on her birthday is appropriate."

"Sorry, babe. I didn't think about it that way. It won't happen again."

Linsey is afraid to taint Kristen's opinion of her new boyfriend, so she never mentions the roses. We forgive and then forget things in our relationships, but those we tell when we are upset remember that shit forever.

Marie is different, though. She is only a work friend. Maybe she will shed some light.

"I tried to warn you. Charles has always been a player," she says. "People change when they meet the right person," Linsey insists.

"Men don't change. Break up with him. Once a cheater, always a cheater."

But maybe it was innocent. Lately, Charles works the subject of engagement rings into their conversations. The following day at breakfast, he asks again, "What shape of diamond do you like?" Linsey's eyes open wide, and she is giddy with the thought.

"I'm not sure."

"Well, think about it. And don't forget I'm flying to New York next week."

"I know. For a haircut."

"Yes, and I can stop by the Diamond District in the afternoon to see what they have in stock before dinner with my cousin, but I may not be able to call much. I'm going to be pretty busy."

"How long will you be gone?"

"I fly home Sunday night. Don't look so sad. I'll leave you some cash to buy a new outfit and take you anywhere you want for dinner when I get back. Make the reservation."

That weekend, Linsey spends hours searching for the perfect dress and posts a selfie in front of the store with the caption, Treat yourself to a taste of luxury #D&G #balharborshops. The post fell short of the number of likes she anticipated, and she zooms in on her imperfections to figure out why.

"My nose is crooked, and my lips are too thin," she tells Charles when he returns.

"Your nose is not crooked."

"Yes, it is. Look!"

"Go see a doctor if you want. I will pay."

The dermatologist Linsey finds begins a subtle transformation. After each nonsurgical procedure, her confidence increases along with the number of selfies she posts. Comments like "You look great" and "Beautiful" only encourage her, and she continues to fixate on her appearance.

She always had her hair highlighted and her nails done. But she purchases an unlimited blow-dry package, convinced the hairdressers perform some hocus pocus with her hair that she can never duplicate. Now we see her twice a week, and she confides in us.

"Linsey, have you been crying?" I ask.

"Why? Is my nose red? I hope it doesn't swell."

"No. It's fine, but what happened?"

"I couldn't find my key to the BMW this morning, and I didn't want to bother Charles at work. He gets so annoyed. So I took his Tesla, and when I looked in the backseat, there was a gift box with a red bow."

I know what she's getting at. We all suspect Charles cheats on her, but I say, "Maybe it's for you."

"No. I just knew Charles didn't buy it for me. I looked inside, and it was lingerie in a Medium. I'm an Extra-Small."

"Oh."

"I want to ask him who it is for, but then what, more lies? If I leave, he will probably move another girl in. I can't be the one tossed aside."

I see the engagement on social media a few weeks later, but is three carats enough to distract her from his infidelities? She needs to ask herself that, and I am the sounding board.

"Marie said I shouldn't marry him."

"What do you think?" I ask.

"I mean, my life is good. Charles said I don't have to work anymore if we get married. And it's not like Marie is so happy being single."

"True."

"I think I need to go home for a visit."

"Good idea."

Linsey waits to speak with her mom in person, never mentioning the problems with Charles beforehand, and it's for the best. She exits the airport rolling a small carry-on bag behind her.

Way too much thought went into packing. Even the understated outfit she has on seems too sophisticated. No one here knows how to dress.

Her mother stays in the car while Linsey opens the passenger side door with an embarrassing screech and tosses her bag into the back.

"Your father needs to oil that door," her mom says with a smile. Then flicks her cigarette out the window and drives away.

Has it been so long that she forgot how different the people here are? Who even smokes cigarettes anymore?

"I'm so excited about the wedding! I have some money set aside," her mother says.

There are several worn envelopes in the bottom drawer of her mother's nightstand, one for Christmas presents and one for emergencies, but there is no way there is enough for the gown Linsey wants.

"Charles said he wants to buy my dress."

"He sounds wonderful. I can't wait to meet him."

Linsey's chest tightens with the thought.

The house is exactly the way she left it. A fine layer of dust covers every surface, and it smells like last night's supper.

"I made lunch for us. Tuna fish," her mom says.

"Do we have any bottled water?"

"What's wrong with the sink water?"

"Nothing. It's fine."

"Dad is outside. Go show him your ring."

Linsey puts the carry-on in her bedroom and goes out the back door where she finds her dad tinkering with his car. He looks up with a smile. "Hey, Skittle."

"Hey, Dad. Mom wants you to see my ring."

"She already showed me on the computer, but let me see it again."

Linsey sticks out her hand.

"Sure is pretty, just like you."

While they eat, Linsey pictures a reception given by her parents. Maybe something like the one they had with a buffet and centerpieces of carnations and baby's breath. She has to figure out how to get out of it before the visit ends.

"Do you want to go with me to the grocery store? I need a few things," her mother asks.

"I'll go for you."

"Are you sure?"

"Yes. I want to drive around anyway."

She passes by the high school and the camp where she was a counselor, and can't help but think about what would have happened had she gone through the pregnancy. The baby would be a little person by now, walking and talking and learning new things, and they would be living with her parents.

There is one spot left to park her mother's car at the end of the lot and she is footsteps from the entrance of the store when someone calls her name.

"Linsey! Look at you, all grown up. I didn't know you were coming home."

"Hi, Mrs. Harrison. It was last-minute."

Mrs. Harrison has a pair of Versace sunglasses that Linsey wishes she had purchased when she saw them online. But Mrs. Harrison is more impressed with Linsey's Missoni sweater.

"That's a beautiful sweater. I don't remember you being such a fashionista when you were younger?"

"I wasn't."

"Kristen tells me you are getting married."

Linsey flashes the ring, and Mrs. Harrison grabs her hand and pulls it closer.

"You didn't choose this, did you?"

"No. My fiancé surprised me."

"I was going to say you wouldn't recognize something like this if you saw it."

"No, I guess not."

"It suits you. And, all that Florida sun has done wonders for your pale complexion."

"Thank you Mrs. Harrison," Linsey says. But the kind words from her best friend's mother don't seem genuine. As she peruses the first asile inside the store, she pictures Mrs. Harrison at the wedding in Charles's ear, nonchalantly criticizing the girl she was before leaving this godforsaken place. Linsey will never return to Lansing, even to visit, and can't wait to leave.

"We want to elope. We are thinking Hawaii," she tells her mother on the way to the airport.

"That sounds very romantic."

Linsey knows it's a relief they won't be paying for the wedding.

After they marry, Charles focuses on new ways to make money.

"Don't wait up tonight. I will be late."

"Again?"

"I am having dinner with a guy who wants me to invest in his company."

"What is it?"

"Corporate renovations. They paint and install new flooring at night after businesses close, locally and throughout the state."

The renovations turn out to be a moneymaker. Still, the newly married couple hardly spend time together between Charles overseeing the furniture store and the late nights supervising the crews on weekends. The one night he does come home early to take Linsey out she is lying on the couch watching Netflix.

"Why do you have a phone if you never answer it?"

"I'm sorry. It's in the bedroom."

"Get dressed, and don't take forever. I'm starving," which translates to Charles not in the mood to wait while Linsey tries on half the closet.

Feeling frazzled, she grabs the first thing she can find—a pair of skinny white pants and a black turtle neck.

"Can you see my cellulite in these pants?" she asks, turning around, back to the mirror. Had she not pointed it out, he would never notice the tiny dimples on the back of her legs, and he wouldn't care. Now he zooms in on the tight white pants and makes a face. Sitting on the edge of the bed, she rips the pants off in two quick motions.

"Please don't tell me you're changing again," he says with a sigh.

Linsey retreats to the walk-in closet, unable to get it together. She wishes she had washed her hair that morning when she showered. At this point, nothing will boost her confidence, so she grabs the jeans and tank top that never let her down.

"All that fuss, and that's what you're wearing?" Charles asks. She could have killed him.

Nearing the end of their time together, Hurricane Irma forms in the Caribbean as a tropical depression. South Florida is in the center of the cone of uncertainty, and the storm is gaining speed as local television stations switch to constant weather updates.

Hair and nail services are not in any hurricane preparedness brochure, but we keep working as long as the clients keep coming.

"Can you stay for one more? Linsey needs a gel manicure," Helene, my receptionist, asks.

"Of course."

"Thank you for taking me," she says when she sits. "We are flying to New York later, and who knows when we'll be back."

"You're leaving?"

"Yes. The forecasters predict a category five hurricane, and we don't want to be stuck here without electricity."

"You might want to check on your flight. I hear the airports are closing."

"We're flying private."

It's always the same. No one rushes to prepare at first, knowing that most storms won't amount to much. But then, when time is of the essence, residents are ready to abandon ship by flying out or driving north to avoid the storm altogether. Leaving too late could mean getting stuck on the highway without a room, and only a select few can fly out on a private plane at the last minute.

We are in the final panic stage, with rain bands already headed our way, when Linsey posts a selfie in front of the steakhouse where they had dinner that night in the city. The caption reads, Yummy.

The storm eventually passes, with raindrops that only spit on our rooftops, but many still lose power from the strong gusts of wind.

"Don't you think it's a little insensitive?" Charles asks.

"What?"

"Posting at the restaurant while friends at home don't have electricity."

"No. They chose to stay."

But as they say, happiness is fleeting.

The police arrest Charles outside a strip club for his involvement in a Ponzi scheme, the real reason he was out all night. That and the girls at the strip club, of course. There is no bond, and he faces years of prison time.

We see Linsey's name on our schedules a few weeks later. My co-workers gather around my desk, knowing my husband works in law enforcement, dying for details on the arrest.

"Do you think her husband is guilty?" Samantha asks.

"All I know is there was an eight-month investigation."

Julie leans in. "I think we should do her services for free until her husband gets out of jail." I roll my eyes. "Really? Charles probably left her with a stash of cash under the mattress."

Julie raises her eyebrows. "The boutique gave her two pairs of jeans because she was always a good customer. It's a mitzvah, Annie."

"Fine," I say, "if you want to."

This little arrangement of Julie's lasts for over a year.

I do her nails every week for free, and nothing changes for her, as I suspected. To look at her, you would think she still has it all. One week, I ask her if she wouldn't mind coming a little later so I can squeeze in another customer, and she refuses, saying she likes her usual time better, and with the court system as slow as molasses, there is no end in sight.

"Are you planning to wait for Charles?" I ask.

"You love someone forever, or you never really loved them," Linsey says, not answering my question. Then I notice the sharp corner of a price tag visible through the sheer sleeve of her blouse and wonder if she's planning to return it.

"Kristen and her husband had a baby. I saw it on Instagram. It looks like my chances for that are over," she says.

"You're still young."

Then Debbie walks up. "Hey, Linsey. Get washed for me when you finish. I'm doing your blow-dry."

"Okay."

"And by the way, I love your bag!"

Linsey grips the handles of the Valentino Rockstud tote and raises them slightly. "It's a new color," she says.

An hour later, searching for my next client, I pass by the front desk. Linsey has a retail product in her hand, and she is trying to check out.

"Do you have another card?" Helene asks impatiently.

"What's the problem?"

"It's declined."

"Impossible."

"I ran it twice."

Linsey opens her bag to take out the matching wallet, and when she does, I see two tubes of our most expensive conditioner floating around inside.

"Here, try this one," she says, annoyed.

Not sure what to do, I keep walking by, and pretend not to notice.

CHAPTER FOUR:

Faye Carrozza

MY CLIENT SUZANNE ENTERS THE SALON WITH PUR-
pose in her step. Her brown hair is loose around her shoulders
and bounces as she walks in the highest heels. Without checking
in with the receptionist or looking around, she comes straight to
my desk, sits down, and says, "Barry and I are getting divorced."

"I'm so sorry. What happened?" I ask, genuinely shocked.

"Barry says he's miserable and wants out."

Suzanne's personality is daunting, but it's nothing new to
her husband. There must be a reason he's choosing to leave now,
and I assume it's for someone else. There is always someone else.
She pulls her hand from my grip and scrolls through her phone
to show me an Instagram post. It's Barry with his arm around a
tall blonde. "Marian?" I ask, shocked. "Isn't she the realtor who
sold you the house?"

"Yes, that was four years ago. And who knows, it could have been going on the whole time."

"You think?"

"Barry says no. They saw each other at a fundraiser a few months ago and began texting."

"It's possible."

"Regardless, I found her on Yelp and ruined her five-star rating."

"Suzanne, why?"

"What do you mean why? She's fucking my husband. I called her a home-wrecker in the review and gave her one star. Barry is pissed. It cost him over five hundred dollars to take it down."

Suzanne has two choices at this point. Take the high road, move on, and maybe find someone more suited to be with her. Or take the longer, darker path and stay stuck. I might have known she would choose the latter.

Barry moves to a luxury condo with an Olympic-sized pool and a five-star restaurant in the lobby by Suzanne's next appointment, and she remains in the marital home. His visitation includes every other weekend with the children from Saturday to Sunday night, giving his ex-wife a whopping thirty-six hours to herself.

She panics as the girls kiss her goodbye, excited to go to new surroundings with their father.

"I don't want that whore around my girls," she tells Barry, but he balks at the order and walks away, saying, "Whatever, Suzanne." Controlling women think their husbands will still listen to them after a divorce, but they one hundred percent won't.

That night Suzanne tosses and turns, picturing the girlfriend cozying up with her husband and daughters like one big happy family. No longer able to lie there, she gets up before dawn, pulls on a pair of sweatpants, and drives over to Barry's, telling herself she will relax once she confirms the girlfriend isn't there.

The twenty-minute drive calms her nerves, and she contemplates getting a coffee after and sitting outside at a small café savoring the morning alone, something she dreamed of doing the entire time she was married. But as she rounds the curve into Barry's parking lot, she immediately sees Marian's Audi. Unable to control herself, she lays on the horn until the man she once married and had children with comes out, his hair ruffled from sleep, or God knows what. A fight ensues, and the police have to intervene.

A judge issues a restraining order and then suggests the couple pick up and return the children to school. And if that isn't possible, find a drop-off point in a public place of mutual distance to transfer the children from one parent to the other.

Starbucks is the meeting spot, and one Sunday, after some months pass, Barry feels brave enough to follow his girls over to Suzanne's awaiting car. Technically he's violating the restraining order but only long enough to speak to their mother.

"I'm just letting you know that Marian and I plan to take the kids to Disney World the second week of October."

Barry speaking this way, as if they are a couple and Suzanne is on the outside, sets her off.

"You aren't taking my children anywhere with that bitch."

"They are my children too, Suze. Please be reasonable."

"Sorry, I'm not sending my daughters away with people I don't know."

"The girls are ten and twelve, and I will be there. Do you think I would let anything happen to them?"

"It's not you that I'm worried about."

"Okay, then you tell them they can't go."

"No. That's on you. You got the girls' hopes up without checking with me first."

As Suzanne drives away, she sees a tear drip from her younger daughter's chin in the rearview mirror. The little girl was eavesdropping as children do, and it bothers her to hear her parents fight, but the real letdown is that she will miss the Disney trip.

Somehow Suzanne can't help pressing further, "Your father didn't have Marian over while you were there, did he?" Together from the backseat, they answer, "No, Mom."

She tells me the story when I do her manicure the following week. "There is no way to know if Barry asked the girls to lie. Why ask if she was there and put them in that position?" I say.

"I just don't understand how the girls can still be nice to him after knowing what he did to me."

"It's different for them, Suzanne. He's their father."

"But they always defend him. What about me? I'm the one who does everything for them, and he gets to have all the fun. If he has enough money to take them to Disney, he should be giving me more."

"What about his girlfriend? Are you ever going to allow the girls to be with her?"

"Absolutely not. I'm going to fight it in court."

"The attorneys are the only winners in that scenario. It's going to cost a fortune to fight."

"Oh well. Barry has to pay the attorneys; if I have to, I will drain every penny he has in his account."

In sharp contrast to Suzanne is Faye Carrozza, another client in a similar situation. She, too, had an ex-husband and two children, a boy and a girl.

My boss, Val, the owner of Indulge Me Salon, first asked me to do her nails some months back. I had heard he was dating the CEO of a high-end furniture brand and knew she would have to be something special to attract his attention. He is older than Faye by about ten years, but his combination of gray hair and tan is most distinguished. He has not one but two failed marriages under his belt, but his kids are grown, and he's ready to settle down again. A lot of life is about timing.

He walks toward my station, holding her hand, "Faye, this is Annie; Annie, this is my girlfriend, Faye."

I quickly see how this classic beauty and Val ended up together. She is upbeat and confident. Her auburn hair is striking and swept up in a loose bun at the nape of her neck, just slightly above the collar of her designer blazer.

He walks away to get them both coffee.

"Your nails are perfect; they only need polish."

"I had a manicure a few days ago, but Val wanted to see me," Faye says and blushes.

"That's so sweet."

Just then, her phone rings.

"Hi, Mom. Yes, tomorrow is a teachers' workday. Yes. I'm sure the kids would love to spend the day with you. Okay. See you in the morning."

I look up for a moment, making eye contact with Faye, but my hands never stop working. It's how I stay on schedule.

"It sounds like your mother is a big help."

"It's my former mother-in-law, but she's is a sweetheart. She's calling to arrange to take my kids to the zoo tomorrow because I have a big meeting at work."

"It's nice that you still have a relationship with her. What about your ex?"

"My ex hasn't paid child support in years, but he's an excellent father, and to me, that's the most important."

The way Faye describes her ex-husband speaks volumes. It takes a lot of self-control not to bash a person you're no longer with, and the difference between Faye and Suzanne resonates with me. Faye's salary gives her some flexibility regarding money. Maybe that's what Suzanne needs, a job so she won't have to rely on Barry for everything, and there is nothing like earning a paycheck to boost a person's self-worth. Later that day, when Suzanne comes in, I casually mention it.

"Have you thought about working?" I ask.

"Now you sound like my ex. Whose side are you on?"

"I thought maybe you could find something fun."

"If I get a job, Barry won't have to pay as much, and I'm not willing to let him off the hook that easy. He owes me over six thousand dollars as it is."

"For child support?"

"For incidentals. The court order says he has to pay half of every extra expense like field trips and dance class and half of any doctor bills his health insurance doesn't cover."

"It must be hard to keep track of all that."

"Not really. I have a spreadsheet."

She needs something to occupy her time besides logging every cent Barry owes her. It's an obsession.

"And if he doesn't take them on his weekend, he must pay for child care. He's not ruining my plans because he wants to be with his girlfriend."

I continue to file and buff her nails.

"Look at my forehead." She tries to lift her eyebrows, but they don't budge. "I got Botox last week."

"You look great," I tell her, and she does.

"Next time, I'm getting filler in my lips, but I didn't have enough cash and didn't want to use my credit card. I'm sick of Barry knowing every penny I spend."

"How does he know?"

"I have to fill out a financial affidavit for the divorce, and if I withdraw cash for anything, I have to log it."

All the more reason, I think, to get a job and make your own money.

"So," she continues, "I started taking cashback every time I shop at Publix. The most you can get is sixty dollars at a time, but only the total for the groceries and the cash shows up on the bank statement."

"That's brilliant," I say.

"I also buy fifty-dollar gift cards to Nordstrom and Saks with my food order so I can shop at the mall with them. There is no way to trace that either."

"Very resourceful."

Suzanne can apply for a job earning six figures like Faye with these skills. But to spite her ex-husband, she refuses to work, ultimately losing the battle to better herself.

One summer afternoon, I wait for Faye at my desk. It's the first time she is ever late for an appointment. I'm looking down when she comes in, and I hear the click-clack of her heels before I see her. "Sorry, I forgot all about my nails and had to get an Uber," she says, still standing. She collapses in the chair, her silk blouse surprisingly still pristine even after being in the heat outside.

"Where is your car?"

"I let my ex borrow it; he broke down on the side of the road for the third time, and he's supposed to pick up our son from soccer practice later."

"That was nice of you." I can't imagine Suzanne talking to her ex, much less helping him out.

"We get along for the kids mostly. I will always care about him, but more like a brother than a husband."

"I get that."

Faye doesn't dwell on her ex. She trusts him to use his best judgment with the kids, and in that way, he never lets her down. Because of him, she can work a demanding job and travel extensively on her time off. And that June, while Faye is off cruising the Mediterranean with Val, things remain the same here. Barry dares to ask Suzanne for a favor.

"Can you take the girls on the Fourth of July weekend?"

"It's your weekend."

"Yes, I know, but I will take them the next two to make up for it, and if you ever need to switch...."

"Why? So, you can go away with your girlfriend?"

"Come on, Suze, let's try to be civil."

"No, Barry, I have plans that weekend."

"Well, my sister said she'd love to watch them if it's okay with you."

"Absolutely not. I told you before I don't want my daughters around your alcoholic brother-in-law."

"You are the only one who thinks he is an alcoholic."

"Let me tell you something, Barry. If I find out they were over there, I will make sure your family never sees the girls again."

Suzanne repeats the story during her nail appointment, and it occurs to me that she, too, needs a love life of her own.

"Maybe you should start dating."

"No way. The men out there are nothing but scum."

"There must be one good one?"

"There isn't."

"If you remarry, you wouldn't need to rely so much on Barry."

"Life is not a fairy tale, Annie."

Suzanne does nothing to help herself, like being stranded on a deserted island and hiding when any possible rescue comes close. Meanwhile, Faye lives a real-life fairy tale with Val. And when I see her next, she is in a hurry to get back to work for an important meeting, so Debbie, blows out her hair at my station to save time.

"I finally bought a new car and gave my ex the trade-in."

"You gave a car to the man who never gives you a penny in child support?" Debbie asks.

"He's driving my kids around. I want them to be safe."

"You're way too good to him."

But Faye doesn't see it like that. In some ways, they are still family.

Both Faye and Suzanne have children graduating from eighth grade a few years later. The venue has limited seating, so each child only receives two tickets for family members to attend the ceremony.

"Who would you like to invite?" Faye asks her daughter.

"You and Dad, but he has to work, so you and Val?"

"I'm sure Val would love to come." And as usual, Faye's positive attitude attracts good fortune, and a friend offers her an extra ticket at the last minute. She immediately calls her former mother-in-law.

"Mom, are you free on Wednesday?"

"I sure am."

"Great. I have an extra ticket to the graduation. We will pick you up at six thirty."

Val escorts Faye and the kids' grandmother into the auditorium at seven that evening, one on each arm. He sits between them in the row, keeping them laughing at his jokes until the ceremony begins.

When I see Suzanne, I ask how she handled the two-ticket limit.

"I sat alone with an empty seat because Barry stood in the back of the room the entire time. Then after the ceremony, he left without posing for pictures with us, and I wanted to talk to him. I found out he's getting married. My fourteen-year-old knew about the wedding plans and kept them from me. I'm so mad right now."

"Maybe she knew you would be upset," I offer.

"I'm not upset they are engaged. I don't like that my daughter didn't tell me. She usually tells me everything."

"She probably didn't know how to handle it." And while Suzanne continues to fret over the upcoming marriage, the salon starts to clear out. She is speaking before working out whatever is bothering her. In this think-talk, she reiterates the worst-case scenario. It's a waste of time when many of her worries never happen.

"If Barry thinks he can take the girls away with her once they are married, he's wrong," she says.

The last blow dryer turns off for the day, and the hairdressers pack up to leave, but Suzanne's voice hasn't yet adjusted to the noise level, and my head is pounding.

I am polishing Suzanne's nails when she spots Faye in the entrance.

"Who is that?"

"Val's girlfriend."

"Did you see her Birkin bag? I guess she's with him for the money."

Val walks up behind Faye, now sitting in the waiting area, and places his hand on her shoulder. She looks up at him, and he kisses her lips.

Suzanne makes a face at me.

"They're gross," she says.

Suzanne leaves, and it's Faye's turn to sit down at my station. I wipe down the surface as Val pulls a chair over to join us.

"Are you hungry, babe?"

"I haven't eaten all day."

"When you finish your nail appointment, I thought we could get a couple of drinks at Vinny's and then have dinner."

"You are reading my mind."

It's like I don't exist, which is fine, but I'm hyper-focused on their personal conversation with nothing else to distract me. I am thankful when the receptionist walks up and breaks the spell between them.

"Can I leave?" she asks.

"Yes, I will close up," Val says. "See you tomorrow."

He walks away to lock the front door and then comes back, and when he does, he rests a hand on Faye's thigh, and now I feel like the third wheel on a very awkward date.

"You said you have something you wanted to tell me," Val says, looking into her eyes, giving her his complete attention. I keep my head down and start to polish.

"Yes. I checked the mail today and received a letter from Support Enforcement."

"Maybe your ex finally paid something?"

"You won't believe it. I got a check for the entire amount owed. It's over eighty thousand dollars."

"How is that possible?"

"He buys a scratch-off lottery ticket every morning, and I guess he finally won. Luckily for me, the state pays any back child support before handing over the winnings."

Val smiles and shakes his head.

"You are a good person, Faye; you deserve it."

CHAPTER FIVE:

Sharon Berkowitz

AFTER HER DELUXE PEDICURE, SHARON BERKOWITZ
arrives at my desk, heels glistening in her Valentino sandals.
"What color did you get on your toes?" I ask, looking down.

"Big Apple Red," Sharon replies. "Not that anyone
will notice."

As a nail technician, I don't get to choose who sits with
me. I am face to face with different types of women every day I
otherwise would have never met, and it is far more interesting
to engage with them than be surrounded by carbon copies. The
clients speak to me as I hold their hands in mine, exposing who
they are. Some don't need to say a word; they are transparent.

After years of seeing the same ones week after week, it's clear
that time management for one is part of someone's personality.
Early clients are always early, and clients who arrive late for their
appointments will always be late. Knowing this and expecting

something different is a waste of energy, and Sharon is always ten minutes late.

I only have twenty minutes before my next client, so I quickly find the matching gel polish in Big Apple Red from the shelf and sit across from her. With her dark hair pulled back from her face, I see how youthful her skin looks. What a shame she became a widow before her time.

When she and her husband bought their seven thousand square foot home, the family of four and their two dogs and one cat fit comfortably inside, but the house seemed vacant after the children left for college and the pets, one by one, took their last breath and were gone.

Condo life sounded good to Sharon, like living in a hotel with someone to valet the car and help with packages. But elevators and the smell of other people's food cooking did not appeal to her husband.

"I don't want to hear anyone's footsteps above my head."

"We could live in the penthouse. It just seems so easy. Maintenance takes care of everything for you."

"It's not like we are cleaning the pool and mowing the lawn. And someday, we will have grandchildren to run around the property."

That was before the heart attack. Sharon's husband collapsed one day at work and died before arriving at the hospital.

After the funeral, everyone moved on. The children live their lives as if nothing happened until something abruptly reminds them of their father. It might be as simple as driving past his favorite restaurant where he sat with his glass of scotch and told them stories about his childhood that start the tears flowing—or seeing a man in a crowded room with their dad's profile. They call their mother at these times, and she comforts them, but who will do that for her?

"I miss his hugs the most," she says, and I think about how alone it must feel to lose a spouse after twenty-five years. Guess the other half or the better half says it all.

Human contact is a basic need, and for many single women who come to the salon the only time someone ever touches them is in the shampoo bowl before a hair service or during a massage in the nail department. Those women come here not for hair and nails but because they're lonely.

"What about the friends you used to have dinner with on the weekends? I ask.

"They call to check on me but never invite me to go out with them. Who wants to go out with a widow? I've become a reminder of how fragile life is."

And it's true. None of the women want poor Sharon hanging around their husbands now that she is single, but they continue to call her primarily out of curiosity and to know what to do when their husbands, God forbid, drop dead.

"Had he been seeing a doctor for regular check-ups?"

"Was there heart disease in the family?"

"Are you going to sell the house? It's too big for you now."

Much to her friends' dismay, she stays living in the house. And when the phone calls get fewer and farther between, she is thankful for her college roommate, who she speaks to every night.

"Are you eating?"

"No. I don't have much of an appetite."

"I understand. When Bob moved out, I lost twelve pounds."

Death and divorce are different, and the former, while more painful, has its upside. No attorneys are fighting over the assets or who will spend holidays with the children. And no bitter spouse blames the cheating one for ripping the family apart. In death, only the good memories remain. It's hard to recall anything negative about a loved one once they pass, especially when they leave behind a small fortune.

Sharon's husband left her well cared for; for that, she loves him even more, and the thought of dating someone else is out of the question. None of the gray-haired sixty-somethings appeal to her anyway. Her husband aged over the years, but she still remembers him as they met so long ago. In her eyes, he hardly changed (one of the perks of a long, happy marriage).

Marriage can be challenging to say the least, but theirs was better than most. The day he died started like any other. Kisses on the way out the door, backing the car out of the driveway, waving goodbye. Except he never came back this time.

Occasionally, she goes out, but she is met with deafening silence when she returns home. Funny, she never noticed the sound the sprinklers make outside or the rumble of the air-conditioning kicking on and then stopping. Little sounds become amplified like never before.

It is easy to imagine her loss. The spot where her husband slept in their king-sized bed is empty, yet she can't bring herself to move to the center. In the half-dream state, just before dawn, she pretends he is lying there, his breath in rhythm with hers. It prolongs the familiar dread that comes once fully awake. Only then does it sink in again; he is gone forever.

His coffee mug is still next to hers in the kitchen, and she doesn't have the heart to let it go. She questions why God would take her husband still in his prime and leave her sister's husband on this Earth. While still very much alive, Marcy's husband, Stanley, in a late stage of dementia, is a shell of the man he once was.

Her sister's only regret is that she didn't divorce him when he cheated years earlier. Had she walked away then, he would be someone else's problem now.

It's always shocking who meets and marries a man and who does not. We have all seen a girl, pretty as a picture, who cannot find a mate, hard as she tries.

Marcy, a dowdy girl, married twice. Stanley, the dementia patient, is her second husband. Had Marcy stayed married to her first, the father of her son, who turned out to be more successful than initially predicted, her life would have turned out completely different. Life is full of choices. In hindsight, the first marriage wasn't even that bad. It was the institution itself that hardly lived up to the Disney version. For the most part, men are the same. It's a matter of which one fits your ideal world the best.

Marcy could not have predicted that Stanley would lose his memory. At first, he couldn't recall who the president of the United States was. Then he accused his wife of stealing misplaced items, and now he barely recognizes friends and family.

He asks the same questions repeatedly: When is he going off to school? When is his mother coming home? What time are they leaving for the concert? His wife quit reminding him of the present and agrees with everything he says. The television is the only thing that keeps him calm. However, it must be loud for him to hear it, and the constant drone drives Marcy insane.

Once in a while, there is a glimpse of the man Stanley used to be. It's like he knows what is happening to him, and tears roll down his face.

A caregiver came highly recommended by a neighbor who went through a similar situation, and Marcy hires the woman to help out on Tuesdays and Thursdays.

Hyacinth, a portly woman with tons of experience, quickly learns Stanley's routine. She comes from the bedroom carrying his soiled sheets and finds Marcy in the kitchen.

"I just opened the last case of gloves," she says.

"We have more in the linen closet. Hey, I could do some shopping if I can leave Stanley with you on Thursday."

"Sure, Stanley and I are good friends. Aren't we, Stanley?" Hyacinth shouts, and he doesn't hear a word with the television blaring.

Marcy has plenty of errands, but they can wait. She is dying for an afternoon at the mall. And while she is at it, she invites a friend she used to work with to meet her for lunch.

She dresses in the morning and makes a mental note of what she hopes to find. A new pair of white pants and a pair of espadrilles would spruce up her wardrobe for spring and a new bag.

Hyacinth has never been late before. It figures that today would be the one time. Marcy is about to crawl out of her skin when she finally comes in through the garage.

"Sorry, the traffic was brutal today. There must have been an accident on the highway, so I had to take the side streets."

"No problem. I think you have everything you need. I made Stanley a sandwich and left it in the refrigerator."

"I'm leaving now, Stanley," Marcy shouts.

His face turns red, and tears pool in his eyes.

"I can't stay here. I don't know anyone," Stanley says.

"This happens every time I try to leave."

"Don't worry. We will be fine," Hyacinth assures her.

There are no empty parking spaces in front of the store, so Marcy lets the valet take her car instead of searching endlessly. As soon as she pushes her way through the double glass doors, notes of fine leather and powdery perfume hit her, and her heart begins to race. Who knows what exactly makes the store smell so heavenly. If they could bottle the scent, it would sell out immediately.

The cars lined up in the parking lot do not match the number of people milling about. The store is never very crowded, like when you go on a cruise ship with thousands of people, and only two are in line ahead of you at the coffee bar.

Where to begin? The aisles are clean and bright, and the merchandise has turned over since her last visit.

She purchases a foundation from Bobbi Brown and a candle from Joe Malone before making her way to the escalator. The second floor has the best apparel for her age, and she doesn't waste time trying anything on. The expensive brands she buys usually run true to size. She makes her selections, and the attractive salesgirl rings up her purchases, then presents the shopping bags to her.

"Your receipt is inside."

"Thank you."

The handbags will have to wait until after lunch. Marcy arrives at the hostess station with only minutes to spare, and her friend Cindy is already seated at a small table in the back.

"I'm meeting a friend," Marcy says and points in Cindy's direction.

The hostess smiles and grabs a paper menu.

"Right this way."

Cindy stands and hugs Marcy.

"I ordered you a glass of Chardonnay."

"Perfect."

"I'm so glad you called. It's been way too long."

The waiter appears with two glasses of white wine.

"Do we know what we're having, ladies?"

"Two croissants with chicken salad," Cindy says, "and I get the check, please."

"No, Cindy, I invited you."

"I want to."

"Thank you. You're so sweet. How are you enjoying retirement?"

"I'm taking an art class and joined a book club. Can you believe it? What about you? How's Stanley?"

"Not good. I better check my phone. I hired a woman to stay with him, and I want to make sure she hasn't tried to call."

Marcy fishes her iPhone out of her bag, and she has six missed calls and two voicemails from Hyacinth. She calls back frantic.

"What's wrong?"

"I think you need to come back, he's upset, and I can't calm him down," Hyacinth says.

"I'm on my way." Hanging up, she turns to Cindy. "I'm so sorry. I should have known this was too good to be true."

The waiter comes back with the order on a tray.

"Can I get mine to go, please?" And while he wraps up her meal, Marcy downs the glass of Chardonnay. Cindy hugs her again, and she turns and walks away.

Even after the wine, her hands are trembling all the way home. Leaving the house is not worth the trouble, so she vows to stay home and make the best of it.

They live right on the Intracoastal Waterway. How bad could staying home be with a view like that? And if going to the mall is no longer an option, Marcy will get better acquainted with online shopping.

Priorities shift when a situation changes. Instead of expensive shoes and bags, Marcy searches loungewear and slippers online and stocks up on pots and pans and enough grocery items to cook at home while she's at it. It's easy, only a click away, and everything appears at the front door like magic.

If this new stay-at-home lifestyle is to work, she needs space of her own. Stanley would have never let her sleep in another room in his right mind, but those days are over.

Marcy claims the guest room. The queen-sized bed has a velvet headboard and a newly renovated marble bathroom with a sunken tub that no one ever used. French doors open to a walkway leading to the pool. The only things lacking are quality linens and towels.

The possibilities are endless, but why not get the best? If she is ever going to spoil herself, now is the time.

When the new bedding arrives, she washes, then irons the duvet and methodically makes the bed. There must be a way to ensure Stanley won't get up and leave during the night. Once already, he made his way down the street in his pajamas. The next-door neighbor had to bring him back. So, just after midnight, she ties his ankle to the bed's footboard before turning in. Then if he tries to get up, she will hear him.

It feels like a cloud between the fresh sheets, and sleep washes over her within minutes. Marcy lies awake in the morning, watching the sun creeping slowly into the sky and illuminating the world.

She finally forces herself up when she hears Stanley stir. His bedding is wet, and she has to bathe him before breakfast.

The gardeners come buzzing through the backyard at twenty past nine. When Marcy worked as a teacher, she never had time to micromanage the landscapers or watch them trudge through the iron gate to manicure the lawn and the surrounding hedges because she was out of the house before they arrived. Life was busy then, but working gave her purpose and a social life. Her fellow teachers are friends, and she misses the camaraderie.

With the yard freshly trimmed and Thursday's forecast sunny and a high of seventy-five degrees, she starts a group text with Cindy and three others from the school to invite them over for lunch. Having company is something to look forward to. They can sit outside away from Stanley. Socializing at home can become the new normal.

"Excuse me, sir?"

One of the gardeners turns off the blower and approaches her. "Yes?"

"Can you replant the flowers in my landscape beds?"

"Sure, I will be back tomorrow morning."

"And also add some gardenia bushes to my pots?"

"You got it."

She zooms in on the patio area. Lounge chairs sit on an angle by the pool, each with a rolled-up fluffy white towel, and the patio table stands under a broad umbrella. Marcy has the perfect table scape in mind. When she looks at her phone again, all four girls have confirmed they are coming.

The following two days are rough. Hyacinth came down with the flu and can't help out, but Marcy is determined not to cancel plans.

Stanley sits quietly on Thursday morning in his recliner with the television on, but he is always at his worst when she needs him to behave. Once she feeds him breakfast and tosses a cake into the oven, he has an accident. More frequently, he can't make it to the bathroom. He needs a shower for the second time that day, then the doorbell rings.

Marcy removes the latex gloves and answers the door. Beth, a girl she hasn't spoken to for months, hugs and hands her a book about living with Alzheimer's. She means well, but there is no time to read. Cindy knows this and gives her a tray of cookies. While she greets them, Stanley sits down in his fresh clothes on the wet spot, and Marcy decides to let him stay like that for now.

Seeing the girls in their new designer clothes makes Marcy regret choosing the cheap Amazon jumpsuit that day that looked so cute online. It fits poorly in person.

"Is something burning?" Cindy asks.

Marcy forgot to set the timer in all the commotion, and the edges of the cake are black.

"Go out back and start on the appetizers," she says to the girls, "I'll be out in a minute."

"Hi, Stanley," they chirp as they pass in front of the television. He leans to the side to see around them without answering.

Carafes of water sit at each end of the table, and a charcuterie board runs down the center, overflowing with goodies. The girls load their plates, and Marcy carries out a bottle of rosé in each hand.

"How are you doing?" Beth asks sympathetically.

"I am getting used to being at home, and I like it," she says with a nervous laugh. Their pity is the last thing she needs right now. When she returns to the kitchen to prepare lunch, she notices the odors lingering in the air. Then, the other two teachers walk up the drive.

"Go around back through the gate!" she calls, waving her arm and redirecting them.

Marcy throws the ruined cake into the garbage and sprays the air. Then quickly chops the lettuce for the Caesar salad and places the chicken on top; the girls can cut the rest themselves.

She carries the salads and Cindy's cookies out on a tray. The conversation stops when she walks up. It's obvious they were talking about her.

Cindy stands and awkwardly takes the tray from her friend. "Let me serve."

A glass of rosé sits untouched at Marcy's place setting. She picks it up and guzzles half of it down. The door to the house is ajar in case Stanley needs anything, and she doesn't get up again, hoping to enjoy the moment. The memory would have to last her during the long days ahead.

Beth looks at the hostess over her sunglasses. "I almost didn't come today."

"Why not?"

"Because you never wished me a happy birthday on Facebook, and I see you on there all the time."

"Sorry, I must have missed it," Marcy says. So much for enjoying the camaraderie.

The visit runs its course, and they all pick up their plates and silverware and head to the house. Luckily Marcy arrives at the back door before the rest because Stanley has removed his pants and is standing in his underwear. The door slams shut before her friends see inside, and Marcy turns around. "Leave everything here on the counter, and I will walk you out through the gate. I need to get back to Stanley."

"Thank you, Marcy. Next time I will bring lunch," Cindy says as she gets into her car. Marcy smiles and waves, relieved they are leaving.

Her sister Sharon calls that night to see how the day went.

"How was lunch with your friends?"

"Never again. It was a disaster!"

Marcy relays every detail of the fiasco like an amateur stand-up comedian and has Sharon hysterical with laughter.

Stanley is asleep in his chair when she finally hangs up, his face slack and his chest barely moving. She can't help imagining that this is how he will look lying in his casket and has a thought. His once healthy appetite remains in the past, along with his memory. If she doesn't feed him, he forgets to eat. It would be easy enough to pull off, starving him to death without anyone suspecting any wrongdoing.

Marcy feels tremendous guilt for fantasizing about such a thing. Sharon doesn't know how lucky she is to be alone.

CHAPTER SIX:

Nancy Bennett

NANCY APPROACHES MY DESK WITH SEVERAL BOT-
tles of polish.

"What color do you think? This one or this one? Or should
I have you do a French manicure?

There is no point in spending ten minutes deciding on a
color before the service. Even after committing to one, seeing
someone else in any other shade causes instant insecurity, and
we must rethink the options. I've tried suggesting colors that are
tried and true for any skin tone, and I have enough experience
to know what will look the best on almost anyone, but insisting
they try one I like can backfire. If they hate it, I have to take it all
off and start over, and they never stop me on the first nail. They
wait until an entire hand has been polished, scrunch up their face
and say, "You're going to kill me, but it's just not me." I will then
remove it, contaminating the perfectly cut and oiled cuticles with

tiny cotton fibers that have now ruined my chances for a flawless application of another color, whatever that may be.

So instead of answering Nancy, I start the conversation.

"What are you doing tonight?"

"I have a date with a guy named Roger."

"Really? I can't believe it."

"I know. I don't remember my last real date."

"Did you meet him at work?"

"Yes. Roger is the youngest attorney in the office."

"I knew when you applied for the job that the lawyers would love you."

"Most of them are old enough to be my father."

"How old is this one?"

"He's a year and a half younger than I am. I never thought he'd be interested in me. He's a frat guy."

"So?"

"Well, he's never been married before, for one, but he knows about Amber, and he still invites me to lunch every day in his Porsche."

"Nice."

"This week, a dozen roses came to the office for me with a card from him that said, *Please have dinner with me Saturday night.*

"He sounds like a keeper. What about Amber?"

"My next-door neighbor Rene will keep her. She can play with her daughter until I get home. Chelsea is her best friend. Right, Amber?"

Amber has the same blonde hair and full lips as her mother. She looks up at us and says, "Right," like a parrot, and Nancy turns back to me. "Is the French manicure out of style? I'm wearing a black dress tonight."

At this point, I'm ready to talk about polish. "French is okay, but I like Funny Bunny by OPI. It's white without being too white and more modern than French."

"Perfect."

"What does your dress look like?"

"Above the knee and fitted."

"It's new?"

"Yes. I bought it this morning at Bloomingdale's."

"I'm sure he will love it. Everything looks great on you."

When Nancy leaves the salon, she rushes home to clean her tiny apartment and do her hair and makeup before the date. In all the hurry, when she finally sits down on the tight leather seat of Roger's sports car, it feels like she's just run a marathon. He closes her door and plops down in the driver's seat. "Ready?"

"Ready."

And they drive away.

Roger is considerate, asking what music she likes and holding her hand the entire drive, but doesn't mention his overbearing mother will be at the restaurant until they arrive.

"I didn't know we were having dinner with your mom."

He laughs. "We're not. My mom has reservations every Saturday night with her friends, but we can go straight to our table when it's ready if you want?"

"No. Let's say hello."

But then he hesitates. "Let's get a drink first." They claim two stools at the far end of the bar.

"Are you nervous about introducing me?"

"Not at all. I'm more nervous about what you will think. My mom and her friends can be a lot to handle."

"I'm not worried," Nancy says. But her palms are clammy.

"Mom, this is Nancy. Nancy, this is my mother, Mrs. Bennett."

"Hello, dear, let me introduce you to my friends, the Blumbergs and the Rosens," she says, pointing to the older couples one at a time.

"Hello," Nancy says, meeting their gaze.

"Did the two of you meet in college? Mrs. Rosen asks.

"No, we met at the office," Nancy says.

"Oh, are you an attorney, too?"

"No. I'm a secretary."

"Where did you go to college, dear?"

Then Roger speaks up. "Our table is waiting. We have to go before they give it away, Mrs. Rosen."

"Sorry," Roger says as they approach the table.

"It's okay."

The waiter hands them a menu and fills their glasses with water.

"I guess I will find out what my mom thinks about you tomorrow. I have Sunday dinners with her."

"Every Sunday? That's so sweet."

But Mrs. Bennett turns out to be anything but sweet.

They drive back to Nancy's apartment complex in a daze after the heavy meal and a bottle of wine. Nancy doesn't want the night to end, but has no intention of inviting Roger in. It is too soon for that. Instead, they sit in the dimly lit parking lot to talk.

"Where is Amber's father?"

Nancy hesitates. Should she be honest and say he went to jail for drug trafficking? Roger was probably never around the type of people she is familiar with, but better to tell him now. He will find out the truth eventually anyway.

"He's in jail."

"For what?"

"Drug trafficking and firearms."

"For how long?"

"He won't be coming out anytime soon."

"What about your family? Do they help you with Amber?"

"My parents both passed away." It is easier to say her father is dead than admit she knows little of him. Her life is starting to sound like a Jerry Springer episode already. Then Roger offers up some information about himself.

"My father passed away when I was in high school, and my mother is a breast cancer survivor. I don't have siblings. It's just Mom and me."

"And you're close?"

"Very."

At midnight, Roger escorts Nancy upstairs after their first make-out session in his car. She waits until he walks away before dialing Rene's number to pick up Amber. Did he notice how out of place the Porsche looks in the dingy parking lot? She hopes not.

Amber must be exhausted because her eyes never open as her mother transfers her to her bed and tucks her in. Nancy quietly washes her face and brushes her teeth. She's dying to get into bed and relive the perfect evening in her mind, which she repeatedly does, but sleep still won't come. Maybe after revealing her past, Roger will lose interest.

But no. The next afternoon he sends a text on the way to his mother's house.

I had a great time last night.

Me too.

Can I stop by on my way home?

Yes, if Amber is sleeping.

I get it.

Mrs. Bennett doesn't cook much anymore but vigorously arranges an assortment of snacks on a platter before him, then orders a seafood risotto for dinner. He is looking forward to a relaxing day watching sports on television, but his mother won't stop with the questions.

"Who was that girl?"

"I told you, Mom, we work together."

"She's not Jewish, is she?"

"No, Mom, she's not Jewish."

"And she has a child?"

"Yes. A girl."

"Where is the father?"

"He's out of the picture."

"You shouldn't date someone you wouldn't marry."

But marry, they would.

"When does the lease end on your apartment?" Roger asks months later as Nancy folds the laundry he brought over from his apartment.

"I have about four months left."

"I don't want you to renew it. I'm looking for a house, and I want you and Amber to live with me."

"I have to set the right example for Amber."

"I agree."

Roger doesn't call his mother to tell her how serious things are, knowing what she will say. He waits until the following Sunday and brings it up over dinner.

"It will never work."

"Why not?"

"She is not from the same type of family that you are."

"That doesn't matter. We are in love."

"Do you want to raise someone else's child?"

"I never thought I would marry or even date someone with a child, but Nancy is the one, and we want to have more children together."

"I'm telling you now that you can forget about using your grandmother's ring if you marry this girl."

His grandmother's diamond ring is far more extravagant than anything Roger could ever purchase on his own, considering he also needs a substantial down payment for a house. He might have known that he must marry a girl with a similar social standing to use the family heirloom. So, he invests in something less expensive.

On a Saturday, the skies above are a crystal-clear blue and reflect bright light into the vast empty homes they stroll through with the realtor, illuminating the finishes. Nancy holds onto Roger's hand, and Amber playfully wedges herself between them.

Nancy dreams of living in a house so big it's possible to get turned around and forget her way, but she never thought she'd own one. Amber takes off running through each bedroom with her imaginary friends, excitedly picking the one that could be hers, but her mother is afraid to get ahead of herself. What if it doesn't happen?

"I like this house the best," Roger says. "What do you think?"

"I love it," she says, but encourages him to make the final decision. "I would be happy to live in any of the ones he showed us."

"Look around again and make sure it has everything you want while I speak to the realtor."

The home can only be described as a mini hotel with room after room of floor-to-ceiling windows and doors. She steps out onto the balcony upstairs to admire the view, and Roger finds her moments later.

"I made an offer, but there are already multiple offers on this one. Hopefully, we get it, but I need to ask you something first."

"What do you need to ask me?"

Roger is down on one knee and pulls the ring out of his pocket. The one-carat solitaire gleams in the sunlight.

"Will you marry me?"

The realtor appears with Amber and a bottle of champagne. He makes a toast "to a life of health and happiness" and wishes them luck obtaining the house they love.

From the car, Roger calls his mom.

"You're on speaker. Say hello to your future daughter-in-law."

"Congratulations to you both. I hope you find true happiness," Mrs. Bennett says flatly.

"Thank you, Mom. We will see you tomorrow around six for dinner."

Nancy looks at Roger when he hangs up.

"Your mom didn't sound thrilled."

"She wouldn't be thrilled with anyone."

"Send me her phone number, please, so I can call her tomorrow."

And in the morning, she calls.

"Hi, Mrs. Bennett. I'm looking forward to dinner tonight. I was wondering if I could bring dessert."

"No, please don't. My girl is making something special."

The dining room at Mrs. Bennett's reminds Nancy of her grandmother's house, the scent of the expensive wool rug and antique wood bringing her back to her childhood for a moment. She never felt any love at her grandmother's, and this house gives her the same unwelcome feeling.

Roger's mother doesn't look at Nancy when she speaks to her and ignores Amber altogether. Then she says, "No one brought me anything? Remember the delicious tarts that Sara used to bake?"

"Yes," Roger answers. Then quickly turns his attention back to Nancy. "Nancy, show my mom the ring."

"Lovely. You must make a fortune at this law firm of yours if you can afford a ring and a house." Then she looks at Nancy. "I suppose I will be paying for the wedding."

"We don't want anything expensive," Roger says.

On the way home, Nancy asks, "Who is Sara?"

"Sorry about that. Sara is a girl I dated in college, before law school. My mom always hoped we'd get married."

Nancy tells herself that she shouldn't be jealous of a girl Roger dated. Everyone has a past. And as far as his mother attempting to make her look bad by not bringing a dessert, she will ignore it. Maybe Mrs. Bennett needs time to warm up. But a few weeks later, at another Sunday dinner, she is at it again.

"What are you planning to wear for the big day?" She asks.

"My cousin, Sandy, in Chicago, offered me her gown."

"Is it traditional to wear a wedding gown for a second wedding?"

Nancy wonders if it is a question that requires an answer or a statement she's making, and ruffles through her purse. "I have a picture of her in the dress." She shows the photo to Mrs. Bennett without Roger seeing it.

"Look, it was beautiful on my cousin."

"You won't be getting married to Roger in that dress!"

"Why?"

"The dress has been worn inside a Catholic Church."

Nancy has no idea what she means, but stays quiet.

"I will set up an appointment to find an appropriate gown for you and a dress for Amber and let you know when it is."

"Thank you, Mrs. Bennett."

When they get back into the car, Nancy looks confused.

"What is her deal with the Catholic Church?"

"I should have warned you about that."

"I don't get it."

"Listen. My mother is not always easy, but let her help you find the dresses. She has excellent taste in clothing. You'll see."

Nancy trusts Roger and arrives early with Amber at the bridal salon. They wait in the car until Mrs. Bennett goes inside.

"Come on, Amber, it's time to go dress shopping. And don't forget we need to be on our best behavior."

The phone rings and Roger's picture shows on the screen.

"I have bad news. We lost the house to a cash buyer."

Nancy has a sinking feeling. What if losing the house was just an excuse to call off the engagement? What if his mother convinced him he could find a girl better suited to him without a child from a previous marriage? But pushing the negative thoughts aside, she collects her precious daughter who anyone could love, and steps inside to try on dresses.

"Hello. I take it this is the bride? And your flower girl?" The owner of the boutique says in a disingenuous drawl.

"Yes, my flower girl and also my daughter, Amber."

"Oh, I see. Well, you can go straight back to the fitting room. Let's find the wedding gown first and then pick out a flower girl's dress."

The owner carries a fluffy white gown across her body to the fitting room, where Mrs. Bennett sits on an oversized chair.

"I thought you'd be early," her future mother-in-law says. But before she can answer, she hears her name called from the other side of a billowy curtain.

"Nancy? We are ready for you in here."

The three dresses hanging there are on another level. The prices are not marked. The quality is unlike anything else, and the gown they all agree on is simple—form-fitting off-white lace with tiny sequins scattered on the bodice. Roger's mother doesn't react, but Amber speaks up. "Mommy, you look like a princess!"

"There is a mini version of the dress that would be perfect for the flower girl." the owner says and taps the keyboard of her computer for an uncomfortable amount of time while Mrs. Bennett stands there stoically.

"The matching dress is in stock in her size, and if you order it today, we should receive it in a few weeks," she finally says. "Should I put it under Bennett?"

"She's not a Bennett."

"Just for the order?"

"She's not a Bennett," she says again.

This lady is too much.

"Let's go outside, Amber," Nancy whispers.

Once outside, the little girl looks at her mother.

"Mommy, when you marry Roger, will your last name be Bennett?"

"Yes."

"And mine too?"

"No.

"Why?"

"You have your father's last name."

Nancy has to figure out how to handle this situation with Roger's mother. Her future is riding on it. Nancy's mother died young without a penny to her name, but she stressed the importance of manners and always acted like a lady. Proper behavior is something money can't buy, and no one can take from you. It all boils down to self-control. You can't just fly off at the handle and tell off the mother of your future husband.

She was also smart enough to know that complaining about his mother to him would not help matters. Mrs. Bennett can twist whatever is said and make it seem that Nancy is the one causing problems. Better to say nothing when Roger calls again. She never has to wait long to speak to him.

"How was dress shopping?"

"We both found dresses."

"How was my mother?"

"Pleased, I think."

"Good. Call me when you get to the apartment, and I will pick you up. The realtor has a few houses he wants to show us."

Had Nancy fought with Roger over his mother, the fighting could last throughout the marriage, driving a wedge between the young couple. Instead, she waves goodbye to Mrs. Bennett as if nothing happened and goes to meet her fiancé, who is ready to purchase the home of her dreams.

Unfortunately, real estate is all about timing. Every house is lacking in some way, and Roger looks frustrated.

"I have the perfect house for you, exactly what you're looking for an hour north of here," the realtor suggests.

"Can't do it. That's too far." Roger says, "My mother lives alone, so we need to stay close to her."

Nancy digs her fingernail into the palm of her hand to keep from rolling her eyes.

"There is one more. It hasn't appeared on the MLS yet. It is a spec home, brand new, and in your price range."

"Let's see it," Roger says.

Though not evident at first, this home is the right choice. It doesn't have a pool or a fancy kitchen, but those things come in time.

They move in the weekend after the wedding, and Nancy finds out she is pregnant with twin girls the following summer.

Preparing the nursery takes all her time. She evolves as a wife and mother of three and enjoys every moment of designing the life she dreamed of because no one comes along and hands you your world. You have to mold it. It helps if you have a clear picture of what you want, not a blurry version of you and your husband living in a mansion but a detailed vision to begin building it.

For Nancy, it included little things she could never afford before, like enough clothing to fill her new custom walk-in closet. And then dream goals like a monotone formal living room that no one ever sits in and a Range Rover in the driveway in black with black interiors.

Little by little, it happens. Roger loves making her wishes come true because she appreciates everything she has. And Nancy loves her life, yet, she has a habit of stashing cash in her closet, even years later, always preparing for the day her fairy tale ends.

Before the firm's annual Christmas Party, the weather unexpectantly takes a turn, and Nancy needs a long sleeve top instead of the camisole she planned to wear initially. Not that there aren't several things already in her closet that would work but the women's department of Saks Fifth Avenue is sure to have something better. The clothes are the perfect mix of conservative and flashy to carry her through anything that comes up in the life of an attorney's wife, like costumes for the occasions. No one ever questions if this girl belongs with her successful husband, but on the inside she remains the single mother from a broken home, and sometimes has a nagging feeling she'll end up behind the desk where Roger found her.

On this shopping spree, she avoids salespeople, plucking hangers from the racks herself and piling her selections on the counter next to the register, delaying the ultimate decision of which one to wear. She never considers herself an addict, never abusing drugs or alcohol, but the amount of shopping at the speed she manages has to be a problem. Yet she can't stop. The only thing saving the shoe department's inventory is a call from the babysitter.

"I'm sorry, I woke up sick this morning, and I don't want the kids to catch whatever I have."

"Okay, thank you for calling."

Immediately she calls Roger at the office.

"We have a problem. No sitter for tonight."

"I will call my mother."

"I don't know if she can handle all three."

"Amber is a big help with the twins."

"True."

Mrs. Bennett shows up early with her purse on her shoulder and her nose in the air. Nancy refuses to call her "Mom," so she commonly avoids any title. They exchange hellos with no eye contact, and together they enter the family room where Amber is playing with the twins.

"Hi, Grandma. Look how I braid my little sisters' hair," Amber says.

"Don't touch them, dear; your hands have germs."

Nancy takes Amber to the side for a warning.

"Please behave for Grandma."

"I will."

"And help her with your sisters."

"Okay, Mommy."

But after the twins are asleep, Mrs. Bennett walks into the kitchen and sees Amber pouring milk into a glass and emptying the carton.

"Don't drink that milk; it's for your sisters," Mrs. Bennett shrieks.

Amber runs to her room and crawls under her bed, muffling her cries with a pillow. She's still lying there when her mother returns.

"What's wrong?" Nancy asks, kicking off her heels and crouching down in her dress pants.

"Mommy, Grandma's not nice to me. She doesn't want me here."

"Come on, get in bed, and I will lay with you until you fall asleep."

"What's wrong? Why was Amber crying?" Roger asks when Nancy comes into the bedroom.

"It was something your mother said to her."

"Really? When I walked Mom out, she told me her cancer is back."

"She did?"

"Yes. And I'm worried this time."

She sure doesn't look sick, but Nancy bites her tongue and wonders if her husband also resents Amber being there. It doesn't seem so. He always includes her when people ask how many children he has; when he prepaid college for the twins, he did the same for her.

Amber feels inferior, too. Having a different last name and knowing she has a father out there somewhere who isn't taking the time to come to see her, whatever the reason, hurts. And naturally, when she becomes a teenager and is at her worst like all teens are, she takes it out on her little sisters, jealous that they don't have any conflict to deal with in their lives.

Nancy is in the hall to the girls' rooms and hears her oldest daughter say, "No one likes you," to one of the twins.

Girls will be girls. And in a perfect world where all three are Roger's natural children, there would still be sibling rivalry and harsh words. Nancy ignores the comment.

"Girls, get ready to go to Grandma's."

It's Sunday. Time to put on a brave face and have dinner with Mrs. Bennett.

"How are you feeling?" Nancy asks her mother-in-law during dinner.

"I need surgery, but I told the doctor I'm not ready."

"You should listen to the doctor, Mom," Roger says.

"Where is Amber?" Mrs. Bennett asks.

"She's finished eating. I think she's on her phone in the living room," Nancy says.

"I don't want her near my bedroom. All my jewelry is in there."

"Mom, why would you say that?" Roger asks, and Nancy shoots her a look.

This time, Mrs. Bennett can't squirm her way out of it, so she holds her stomach and leans back in her chair. "I'm in such pain tonight," she says, and the subject drops.

When I see Nancy at the salon, I wonder if she still lets Mrs. Bennett torture her.

"Are you going to your mother-in-law's house for dinner tomorrow?"

"Not this week. Roger is taking the twins, and I am going shopping with Amber. I need a dress for a New Year's Eve party."

"I thought you bought a dress for that."

"I did, but I think I can do better."

"So you have to return it?"

"No. I never return. I hate how the salespeople look at you like you can't afford it."

The following summer, Sunday dinners end abruptly. Sure Mrs. Bennett was seventy-six years old and diagnosed with cancer for the second time, but the quick exit she makes from life here on Earth seems way too easy. Nancy was expecting a long, drawn-out, fading slow kind of death, not one like this.

"Amber, wake up. Grandma passed away in the night."

"Really?"

"Yes. It was her heart."

"She doesn't have a heart."

PLEASE DON'T REPEAT THIS

"Amber!"

"Mom, you know you were thinking the same."

And although Nancy will never admit it, she is thinking the same. Her husband has to be heartbroken, though. Losing both parents makes you an orphan of sorts.

No one is leaving the house, so Nancy puts a brisket in the oven over some peeled carrots and potatoes, so that by the evening they can all enjoy a home-cooked meal.

The girls are treading lightly, letting their father grieve the loss, but Nancy can't bring herself to cry. There is no one to judge her every move anymore.

She needs to figure out what to wear to the funeral, and with that thought her heart rate starts to climb. There are always so many eyes on her. Usually, she'd be out searching for a black ensemble all the mourners would envy when duty calls, but she can't bring herself to leave Roger home with the kids at a time like this, so she enters her closet to see how dire the situation is.

Not so long ago, she didn't own one good dress. Now she has more than one person could ever need. Whichever she chooses, it will be the last time she wears it, never able to reuse anything previously worn at a funeral. She is pleased to find that a dozen or more appropriate dresses, half with the tags still attached, sit in her closet already.

She hangs one aside, a knee-length Chiara Boni La Petite Robe, and scans the shelves for a black bag to go with it. Her handbags are not on display like in an episode of *Cribs*. They sit wrapped in their dust covers on an upper shelf. The total number never used or forgotten entirely shocks her once she sees them laid out on the floor. One of the original purchases bought early on as an anniversary gift from Roger is still her favorite. So why does she need all the others? Seeing them together makes it easy to decide which ones are special, and literally, the rest can go.

For so many years, shopping was like a full-time job. Constantly searching for the perfect item at the best price only to never use it left Nancy exhausted and riddled with anxiety. And what is the point in keeping a dress that cost five hundred dollars only to cringe at a waste of money it was every time she looks at it? Not to mention the waste of time it took to find it. She begins by placing the unused clothing and accessories into trash bags, only stopping for water breaks and a granola bar, and it still took seven hours to organize the remainder and put it all away.

This clean-out and the revelation that came with it may have never happened if she wasn't in mourning, trapped at home. When she finishes, the remaining items have plenty of space between the hangers, allowing each garment easy access. From then on, she shopped only with intention, not on impulse.

On the way to the funeral, Nancy notices they are heading opposite where they should be.

"Don't we have to take I-95?" she asks when Roger passes the entrance to the busy highway.

"I have to stop by my mother's house first."

Inside the car is an unusual silence. The three girls are unsure how to behave on such a day as this.

Roger parks in the driveway next to Mrs. Bennett's car. "Wait here."

It is hard to believe she is gone. There are things Roger will need to sort out as an only child, like the house and all the contents, but Nancy will be there to help.

When he still hasn't come out fifteen minutes later, Nancy finds him searching for something in his mother's bedroom. What could be so important?

"We need to go," she says.

Finally, he opens a drawer and comes across the little red box he is after.

That night, when all is said and done, Roger hands the box to his wife. "I know my grandmother would have wanted you to have this ring."

Nancy moves her diamond eternity band from her left hand to her right and slips his grandmother's ring on her finger. She has never seen anything so beautiful, and it fits her finger perfectly. Why did she ever doubt Roger's devotion?

I immediately notice the ring when I see her. You can't miss it.

"Nancy, this ring! When did you get this?"

"I inherited it from my mother-in-law."

"I heard she passed. I'm sorry for your loss."

"We weren't close."

"I remember."

"How many carats is it?"

"It's over four."

"I think you earned it."

"I sure did."

CHAPTER SEVEN:

Valerie Martin

AS I ENTER THE SALON, THE RECEPTIONIST, VALERIE, looks up and beams her smile at me from behind the front desk. Her dark hair is pin straight today, and she's wearing a skimpy tank top with a blazer to keep it professional. A long line of clients waiting to pay and make future appointments stand before her.

"Can you do my nails tonight?" she asks, leaning to the side as I walk past her.

"Yes, after my last client."

"Thank you, Annie."

The receptionist position is more than accepting payments and answering phones. Valerie, naturally gregarious, makes every client feel pampered, remembering names and going out of her way to accommodate customer requests. That's the goal. There is a salon on every corner; if we can't satisfy our customers, the next one will.

Valerie's meager salary barely covers the cost of her high-end makeup and the lip gloss she constantly reapplies, accentuating her naturally full lips. Luckily, she doesn't need the money.

Before she started working with us, Valerie already had the life of her dreams. She lives in an upscale neighborhood with tree-lined streets overlooking a sprawling golf course and drives an E-class Mercedes that her husband, Craig, bought her as a push present when their son Noah was born. But with all this, she still isn't content. That's the thing with getting everything you want. It may not be what you thought.

Noah was sleeping soundly at nap time in his crib upstairs. Valerie quietly checked her missed calls from the velvet sofa in the living room, hoping to hear from Craig. Even a text would show her husband thought of her during the day, but nothing.

She pulled the plush throw over her feet. The chilly air from the vent above turned them to ice, but she felt too weighed down by her situation to move. Her book lay just out of reach on the coffee table, but she couldn't pick it up. There is nothing like reading to distract from ordinary life for a moment. Still, concentrating on the romantic story and letting it take her away to another world would be too much of a reminder that romance was missing from her own.

All anyone wants is to be appreciated. If Craig came home after work excited to see her and the baby instead of stopping by the bar for a drink with friends, it would show they were his priority. Valerie needed to find happiness some other way. She contemplated her options, and working outside the home seemed like the one that would save her, the perfect excuse to leave the house every day and gain some independence.

The receptionist job, challenging at times, dealing with demanding clients and the entire staff, has its perks. As the first impression of the salon, she can wear whatever she wants as long as it's stylish and professional. Valerie sets aside the young mom's uniform of workout gear and chooses from the high-end wardrobe hanging in her closet, begging for attention. Immediately the employees fawn over Valerie, knowing she can make or break them, recommending and booking clients with who she sees fit. So the hairdressers blow out her hair, the makeup artists work their magic on her, and I have the pleasure of doing her long acrylic nails every other week.

We spend the hour talking while I file and buff the unnatural-looking tips of her nails into perfection.

"Isn't your birthday coming up?" I ask.

"Yes, it is."

"Thirty-two?"

"Thirty-three."

"What are your plans?"

"I made reservations for dinner at Abe and Louie's on Saturday night."

"I love it there. Who is watching Noah?"

"I'm working all day, and Craig is playing golf, so my sitter will just stay."

Before leaving the salon on Saturday, Valerie has her hair blown dry, never losing hope that she is going out for her birthday. A new LBD hangs in her closet, ready to throw on, but as soon as her husband stumbles up the long, paved driveway an hour late, it is clear they will be staying home. It isn't the first time he has come home drunk after golf and will need to sleep it off. While they argue in the bedroom, the babysitter pretends to believe a case of sunstroke caused the sudden change in plans and quietly lets herself out. Craig continues to drink late into the night, and she knows from experience that he will be useless the next day.

It is no wonder that Valerie strays.

She refuses to sit at home and wait for her husband to resurface Sunday afternoon with a hangover, so instead, after breakfast, she packs the trunk of her car and heads toward the beach with her son. The fresh air tousles the ends of her dark shiny hair with the windows partially open, and the car's motion puts Noah to sleep. At a red light, Valerie looks down at her abdomen. The pregnancy did a number on her body, but you can hardly tell she has given birth anymore. She is still curvy, but the swimsuit, designed to pull the soft area of flesh inward, leaves it smooth as before.

In high school, she had her pick of the awkward teenage boys her age but never dated until her senior year, when her manager took an interest in her. He was a few years older and married, and if it were a decade later, the girls who worked in the restaurant might have reported his inappropriateness. But his youthful good looks somehow allowed him to remove his wedding ring and flirt like he was single. And out of all the scantily clad high school girls that served burgers and seafood on the dock of this casual waterside eatery, he chose Valerie.

They never went out together in public. The relationship consisted of the two disappearing into the restaurant's tiny office once every shift, where the boss groped Valerie's young, innocent body. And in return, he paid her car payment for her, most likely out of the register. Since the wife never once showed up there, it was easy to forget her and not feel guilty for sleeping with her husband. Then while Valerie was away at college, he left the restaurant, and no one ever heard from him again, but her heart still raced when she drove by the establishment, remembering his touch.

It's been years since she allowed herself to think about those days. Engrossed, she almost forgets about Noah in the backseat of the car and her life now. But seeing her son's little face in the rearview mirror snaps her back into the present. Maybe it was a mistake to return to the beach where so many sordid memories live, but here she is now.

A dark cloud hovering above and the ocean breeze keeps the temperature pleasant for a time. Noah plays with a yellow plastic shovel, scooping sand from one pile to another, while his mother patiently waits for the cloud to pass and the sun to warm her skin.

Something makes her look up and notice a familiar face next to the walk-up window where hungry beachgoers purchase hot slices of pizza on the boardwalk. Could it be Troy, one of the young busboys from the restaurant?

His shoulders are broader, sure, and his chest has filled out since then, but his playful brown eyes are the same as always. Troy overlooks her as he makes his way to the ocean for a swim. She imagines that he has forgotten her entirely since it has been so long, or maybe she changed beyond recognition, but on his way back, their eyes meet, and he pauses on the sand.

Saltwater drips off the ends of his sun-bleached hair and runs down his tanned body.

"Valerie?"

She smiles. "Hi, Troy."

"I heard you got married. Is this your little boy?" he asks, bending down to look at her son.

"Yes, this is Noah."

"Hi, Noah. Wow. Valerie is a mother. That's wild. You were always a knockout, and the prettiest mom I've ever seen."

"Aww, Troy, that's so sweet of you."

He stands with his back to the sun, which is now beaming, until finally, he says, "Hey, can I get you a beer?"

College is probably the last time she had a beer, but it sounds good.

"Sure," she says.

He goes away and comes back with a clear plastic cup in each hand, filled to the brim. The sand rises and dips under his feet, almost sloshing the foam over the sides before reaching Valerie, who takes one of the cups, freeing him. "Thank you," she says, and her wide smile lights up her entire face.

"I brought a few extra cups, so I can build a sandcastle with Noah."

He picks up his beer, revealing several in a stack.

An entire sandcastle city is constructed near the shoreline until the sun changes positions in the sky and sunbathers gather their belongings to go home. Valerie has a sinking feeling when she notices the time.

"I need to get going," she says.

"Let me help you."

And together, they walk to the boardwalk, where Valerie rinses Noah off in the showerhead and wraps him in a clean, dry towel.

"He's going to sleep well tonight."

"Can I text you?" Troy asks.

Valerie runs her long acrylic nails through her hair like a comb.

"Sure. Give me your phone, and I will add my number."

She wonders how long it will take for him to text. Will he think texting too soon is desperate and wait, or will waiting too long ruin the momentum? As she passes US1, she feels the slight vibration of her phone along with the familiar ping.

I can't stop thinking of you.

Those words, not a vow or a promise, are enough to make some girls risk everything.

I notice Valerie's skin darker than usual, giving her face a healthy glow the next day.

"Did you go to the beach this weekend?"

ANN CEDEÑO

"Uh-huh. Yesterday."

"With Craig?"

"No, he had a hangover and slept the entire day. Never marry someone thinking you will change them."

"Why? Did he always drink like that?"

"He partied a little too hard when we were dating, and I should have recognized the signs. Anyway, I took Noah to the spot I used to go and ran into an old friend. He bussed tables when I worked in the restaurant. Now he's a bartender."

Valerie has a faraway look in her eyes.

"He lives right on the beach, and we've been texting. I might drive down there to see him later."

"Really?"

"Yes. Don't say anything. I said I have a dentist appointment when I came in."

"Okay, don't worry."

Valerie pulls up to the beach, still in her work attire, scanning the boardwalk for Troy. They meet in the parking lot, and he drops into her passenger seat, smelling of sunscreen, his hair messy from sleep. The heavy door makes a whoosh sound when it closes, encapsulating the two comfortably inside.

"You look amazing," he says, staring a beat too long, "Turn here and follow the road to the end."

The narrow street leads to a small apartment building, and she finds herself walking up a flight of stairs behind a guy she barely knows. Her behavior is risky, but the possibility of finding love, no matter how unlikely, keeps her from turning around and leaving. Unfortunately, Troy's time and attention are the only things he has to offer.

He opens a beer over his tiny kitchen sink, takes a sip, and hands it to her. A barely audible radio plays in the background, and the room smells like salt and sea air, or maybe the ocean view suggests the scent. The sparse furniture and plain white walls take her back to her first apartment and how simple life seemed then.

"Where is Noah?"

"He's with my mom today."

"When do you have to pick him up?"

"In a few hours."

Troy leans over and kisses her; whatever is lacking in her marriage is captured in that apartment. All summer, I hear the details while I do her nails.

"We constantly text when we are not together."

"When does he work?"

"A few nights a week. Enough to pay rent on the apartment."

I finish buffing her nails and lift my gaze. "What color do you want?"

"I'm thinking pink to match my new bathing suit and cover-up, but I dread this weekend."

"What's going on?"

"It's my fifth wedding anniversary, and Craig booked the Breaker's Hotel. I don't even know why I'm going. He's planning to golf all day Saturday. What am I supposed to do?"

"You could relax and read a book."

"I guess. But I would rather be there with Troy."

"I know you would."

When they arrive at the resort on Friday, she longs to call Troy but Craig hangs around, even shopping in the exclusive boutiques by her side. He purchases several things for her, including a pair of Gucci sunglasses. He could never be bothered when she wanted him there, but her attempts to ditch him now and wander around alone are unsuccessful.

They walk through the pool area, drop her packages off in the room, and wait until the time comes for their couple's massage. Then they make their way to the spa, changing into fluffy white robes, and enjoy mini yogurt parfaits and herbal tea in the waiting area.

Craig seems agitated, and when a masseuse offers to escort them back to the massage room, he says he will "be right back."

"Where did you go?" Valerie whispers when he returns.

"To the bar."

"Can't you wait until we finish?"

"I'm on vacation."

Afterward, by the pool, waiters dressed in black Polo shirts and black shorts hover around, and as soon as Craig's glass of Grey Goose dips below the midway point, they swipe his card and refresh it.

He stumbles back to the room, his tab hundreds of dollars higher, and after a few tries he manages to open the door with the room key, then passes out on the bed with the television on, where he stays.

Valerie let the warm water wash over her in the shower until the steam makes her dizzy. Steadying herself, she plucks a towel from the stack and returns to the room to dress and put on her makeup. And if Craig thinks she will spend the evening listening to him snore, he would be wrong.

Her evening bag contains the room key and her phone. She slings it over a new knit dress that accentuates her curves and slips out the door with her hair still damp.

The elevator doors open to the lobby, and Valerie steps onto the colorful Persian rug leading to the front desk and the restaurants beyond.

"I have a reservation for seven."

"Room number?"

"765."

"Table for two, Mrs. Martin?"

"No, only one."

"Of course. Your table will be ready momentarily."

Stepping aside, she pulls her phone from her bag to text Troy. The food smells delicious, and suddenly she is starving.

She giggles at something Troy writes, and Craig comes up behind her.

"Why didn't you wake me?"

Valerie's phone drops to the floor.

"I thought you would sleep all night," she says and bends down to pick it up off the carpet.

"Who are you talking to?" he asks, reaching out for her to hand her phone over.

"No one. Are you crazy?"

But before things escalate, they are interrupted by a staff member.

"Your table is ready, Mrs. Martin." Then he turns to Craig. "Will you be joining us also, Sir?"

"Yes, I will. I'm paying the bill."

The fine dining in the candlelit room can't hide the couple's angst. The palpable tension and the uncomfortable glances at one another have the waiters serving quickly to avoid any more awkwardness. After dinner, they walk back to the room in silence and turn in for the night.

"I'm going down to the shops," Valerie says in the morning.

"Can we eat first?" Craig asks.

So together, they enter the dome-shaped dining room. There is a tenderness to Valerie's breasts that she only felt one other time. When she was pregnant. She discreetly brushes the side of her bra with her upper arm to ensure it isn't her imagination, but then the smell of the eggs turns her stomach, confirming her fear.

Monday morning, Valerie calls in sick to the salon and drops Noah off at preschool like any other day. The cool morning air and low humidity promise a perfect beach day and she can't wait to spend it with Troy. On the way, she stops at the store to get a pregnancy test. Getting excited about another baby in this precarious position would be wrong. Yet, the idea of having a baby with Troy, the ultimate romance, has its love-story qualities.

He meets her in the parking lot and carries her chair to the water.

"I need to go to the bathroom," Valerie says, walking the other way.

She comes back with a puzzled look on her face.

"What's wrong?"

"I'm pregnant."

Troy is smiling.

"I hope it's mine," he says.

"Of course, it's yours. Craig never sleeps in our bed," which was mostly true.

Valerie is not a skinny girl. It is months before anyone notices the baby bump. Then in her second trimester, she gives her two-week notice at the salon. I will miss working with her, but she continues having her nails done with me, and we begin counting down the weeks until the birth of her second baby, a girl this time.

With her days free, she spends more time at the beach, and when the torrential downpours arrive in the late afternoon, she and Troy are cuddled up in the beach apartment, dreaming of a future together. They both make promises they can't keep, hers to leave her husband and his to financially support Valerie and the kids. Neither will ever happen.

She has an appointment with me the day before the baby shower.

"Are you sure it's Troy's baby?"

"Positive."

"What are you going to do?"

"Nothing. I can't leave Craig. I need the health insurance."

"Do you think he will suspect anything?"

"I hope not."

And as she opens the last baby gift at the shower, Craig shows up with a bouquet of pink roses for the mom-to-be. As the only person in the room who knows this baby isn't his, I feel uncomfortable. But she accepts the flowers graciously and kisses her husband to the clinking glasses and cheers of the other guests.

A few days after her daughter, Sydney, is born, photos of Valerie and Craig with Noah and the baby are on social media. All in an attempt to save face. But the affair isn't over.

Valerie brings the baby to the beach to see Troy every week. They push the stroller along the boardwalk, play in the ocean, and eat lunch together in the apartment. A few regulars at the beach assume they are a family. Valerie holds Troy's hand on the boardwalk, never thinking she might run into anyone she knows. How careless to let her guard down!

One afternoon Sydney falls asleep on a blanket under an umbrella. They hate to wake her, but it is time to leave to pick up Noah from school.

"I will get your car," he says, picking up the keys from the side pocket of her bag.

And she waits for him to return.

Her car comes toward her a few minutes later with Troy behind the wheel. She doesn't notice her sister-in-law watching from afar. Troy straps the baby safely inside, then passionately kisses Valerie on the lips before she drives away.

Her phone rings, startling her. It's Craig's sister.

"Who is that guy?"

Valerie looks around.

"Where are you?"

"I'm here. At the beach. I saw you."

But how much did she see? Valerie wipes her sweaty palms on the fabric of her dress, then places them back on the steering wheel and swallows hard.

"He's just a friend. We used to work together when we were young."

"He looked like more than a friend."

"He's not."

"I don't think my brother would approve of a guy you used to work with hanging around his wife and daughter. And by the way, he looks like trailer trash."

"Seriously though, we will not mention this to him, will we?"

Valerie is visibly shaken when Noah hops into the car and touches the sand that accumulated into a tiny mound in the corner of the floor mat.

"Why don't I go to the beach anymore, Mama?"

"You're big now. You have to go to school and do homework."

"But I like the beach, and Troy will miss us if we don't go."

"He will be fine."

Her two worlds colliding is a wake-up call.

When I see Valerie the following week for her appointment, she shares what happened.

"I never thought Noah would remember Troy. It's been forever since he's seen him."

"I wondered what will happen when Sydney starts talking. What if she mentions him to Craig?"

"It won't be a problem because I'm not seeing Troy anymore."

"Because of your sister-in-law?"

"It's pointless, Annie. I can't keep doing this. Troy will never step up and take care of us, and if Craig finds out I could lose everything. I'm exhausted, and love is not enough anymore."

I go to Sydney's dance recital when she turns seven. Craig is golfing in a tournament, so Valerie gives me his ticket for the matinee show. Maybe because I know Troy will be there, I spot him a few rows back, sitting with his mother. I would have recognized him anywhere. His face is identical to Sydney's.

When his daughter comes offstage, Troy stands and claps. Sydney politely smiles back with faint recognition.

"Mom, who's that guy?" Sydney asks.

"He's an old friend."

"Do I know him?"

"You used to, a long time ago."

When the auditorium empties, I stay with Valerie while Sydney poses for pictures with her dance class.

"She has no idea, right?"

"No, she thinks Craig is her father, and it's better this way. They are very close."

"Has he stopped drinking?"

"He hasn't stopped exactly, but he's slowed down. Who knew he would mature so much after Sydney was born. He even calls from work now to ask how my day is going. I'm glad I never left."

"Will you ever tell her the truth?"

"Never. What people don't know can't hurt them."

And to this day, Sydney still has no idea.

CHAPTER EIGHT:

Leslie Simmons

SOME CLIENTS TAKE LONGER TO TRUST THEIR NAIL tech than others, but Leslie Simmons is an open book from day one. She talks nonstop about herself and speaks over me when I try to chime in, so I take advantage of the one-way conversation and do what I do best. I listen.

"I don't know why I'm telling you all this," Leslie says, but then lets me into her world, where her life seems pretty perfect. There are only two things she wants and doesn't have: straight hair and a baby.

Hours are wasted in the salon having her hair blown dry and ironed to no avail. As soon as the door opens to the humidity outside, her golden-blonde spirals spring up from memory. Still, she continues to fight the constant battle.

The second wish doesn't come easy either. After years of trying to have a child of their own, she and her husband adopt a baby. Like most couples, adoption is not the first choice but rather the last resort, and raising the little bundle handed to her one morning with only a few weeks' notice proves to be a challenge.

The baby they name Brian sleeps quietly in his nursery while his new parents stand over him. Leslie wonders if mothers are instantly in love with their children or if bonding with them takes time. The baby's tuft of dark straight hair and dark eyes are not what she pictured when she dreamt of a baby. She would have preferred a girl with blonde hair and fair skin like hers and worries she will look like a fraud trying to pass this baby off as her own.

The nanny, a sturdy woman from Jamaica, barrels into Leslie's life.

"Where are the bottles and diapers?" she asks with an accusing tone since most first-time parents she encounters are clueless. Leslie leaves the room and returns with the few items supplied by the hospital.

"We will need more than this."

She makes a list of items for Mr. Simmons to get from the store. Watching the nanny handle the baby, Leslie feels insecure. Swaddling and comforting such a fragile little being is something she has no experience with, yet the nanny does it effortlessly.

"Would you like to bathe him?" the nanny offers when Leslie appears in the bathroom doorway.

"No. I have to go out for a while. I have a ton of things to do."

But the truth is that letting the only capable adult in the house feed, burp, and dress her son works best for Leslie.

She had no idea what kind of father Mr. Simmons would be when she married him. No wife ever does. And whether he is out of his comfort zone or because the baby is not his flesh and blood, he barely participates in caring for his son.

A simple outing requires a professionally packed diaper bag, and the latest stroller needs a YouTube video to open and close properly. It's easier if the nanny accompanies Leslie everywhere they go, and it takes several months before the mother and son finally have alone time outside the house. Other babies are content to sit in their strollers while their mothers proudly parade them around the mall, but Brian never stops crying.

"Maybe he's hungry," a stranger suggests after his wailing gets out of control, and Leslie takes it as criticism. She goes home, and Mr. Simmons finds her crying. "He is constantly fussy, and I don't know what he wants."

"Let the nanny take care of him," he suggests. "That's what we pay her for."

But none of the nannies ever last long. Several come and go before Brian starts kindergarten, and each says they have never met such a strong-willed child.

The frustrated mom receives notes from Brian's teachers in elementary school and phone calls from instructors at extracurricular activities. He has a combative nature and doesn't respect authority. Just once, Leslie wants to be the one to brag the way her friends do, as if they were solely to blame for their children's accomplishments. One of Brian's nannies thought much of it was luck, claiming children were born with certain traits. "They get it at the factory," she would say, and if that statement is true, nothing they do will change the outcome.

As he grows, the problems only escalate, so they seek help with weekly therapy sessions and read books on raising teens, but none of the advice makes sense to Leslie. Her son will hate her if she takes away what matters most: his computer, video games, and iPhone. Instead, covering up becomes her go-to parenting skill. Even after he steals money from her wallet, she never tells anyone, desperate to hide their issues with him.

Occasionally, the couples they socialize with have trouble with their kids, but they have no idea what happens in the

Simmons household. After raiding the liquor cabinet, Brian steals the car one night and drives it into a tree only a block away from the house. Leslie runs to the scene, jumps into the driver's seat before the police arrive, and claims the accident is her fault.

"I'm not sure if covering for him is the best thing," her husband says.

"I had to. If the police knew it was Brian, he would never get a license."

Punishment only makes things worse. When they ground their son, he sneaks out. And they suspect he is experimenting with more than alcohol.

Brian is a good-looking boy, and the Simmons surround him with well-behaved kids in a top-notch private school to influence him to do better. But there he meets Trevor, another troubled teen. The campus is a dumping ground for students expelled from public school for one reason or another.

The two boys become fast friends with easy access to Trevor's older brother's supply of prescription painkillers. They began taking the drugs for fun and distributing them to friends. Eventually, they are caught at school and are asked not to return. Leslie's closest friend, Gayle, calls the following day.

"We are having a girls' lunch. Why don't you join us?"

"I don't know. I was hoping to get Brian to his therapist, but she can't see us until next week."

"Don't shut us out, Leslie. Maybe we can help." It is true. So many parents are too embarrassed to talk about their kid's issues, and often, their friends can be of support.

Rows of dresses hang ready to wear in Leslie's closet. She selects Diane von Furstenberg with a geometric print for this lunch. The only positive thing is that her weight hasn't been an issue since the trouble with Brian. Stress is the best diet. Mr.

Simmons is on the phone, and her son has locked himself inside his room when Leslie leaves to meet the girls.

It's bright and sunny when her Jaguar pulls out of the garage, but she is driving through a downpour twenty minutes later. The sudden change in the weather is typical in Florida. The trunk of Leslie's car has an umbrella in case of rain and a hat to protect her face from direct sunlight that may wreak havoc on her delicate skin. As the vehicle approaches the valet, the sky is clear again.

A gentleman holds the door open for Leslie, and she runs inside the air-conditioned restaurant, afraid the steam rising from the pavement from the brief rain shower will frizz her hair. Her girlfriends are already seated, but Leslie slips into the bathroom to check herself in the mirror. Gayle, dressed in a pink slip dress and nude Saint Laurent sandals, waves her over from a round table when she comes out.

She walks through the crowded room and bends down to air-kiss each girl while securing her Dior bag tightly to her hip with one hand. The scent of her friends' expensive perfume and makeup makes her dizzy, and she drops into the only empty chair. As if on cue, the waitress walks up.

"Are we drinking?"

"Yes, and we ordered appetizers for the table," Gayle says.

"All right. I'll have a Cosmo."

It is noon, and the restaurant buzzes as Leslie tells the girls about her son among the clinking glasses, the spinach dip, and the baked Brie appetizer.

"His therapist mentioned that a personality disorder might explain our trouble with him. She thinks it may be hereditary."

"That's the problem with adoption. You never know what you will get," says Tracy, a brunette with a diamond tennis necklace that sparkles from across the table.

"At the time, the attorney in charge of the adoption assured us he came from a good family."

"They'll tell you whatever they have to."

It is true. It turns out that Brian's birth parents both had problems with addiction and met while in a treatment center.

Leslie only picks at her salad with a fork, and no one notices the plate is hardly touched when the waitress clears the table. Another round of drinks comes before Jeana confesses that her sister had a similar situation with one of her sons. The solution was a boarding school in Utah.

The Simmons considered sending Brian away in the past but knew he would never agree to it. Mr. Simmons finds the number and speaks to an administrator.

"We have seen plenty of boys in your son's situation excel after our program."

"The problem is that Brian will not go willingly."

"Don't worry. If necessary, we handle transportation."

At three a.m. a week later, two burly men in a van pull up to the Simmons residence and yank Brian out of bed. This tactic to stun the teen out of sound sleep makes it easier to get him to comply. He is too confused and intimidated by the men to put up the fight his parents expect. He leaves the only home he's ever known in a hoodie and jeans with his shoes untied.

Leslie and her husband lie awake on opposite sides of the bed, not comforting one another but alone with their thoughts.

Leslie craves every parents dream, to raise a responsible human who they can be proud of, and dreads running into people now and explaining why her son is in school in another state. In every imaginary scenario, she sounds weak and pathetic, and fears that people will think her a failure as a parent.

She dozes, but at seven, she wakes with a start when the front door closes with a click. Mr. Simmons left for work at the usual time as if nothing had happened. The ability to separate himself from the problems at home and escape to the office is enviable. Unfortunatley, Leslie has nothing else to focus her attention on.

The sun comes into the bedroom in tiny strips under the blackout shades, and no longer can she lie there with this giddy feeling of being let free. With Brian gone, the house no longer feels like a prison. She gets up and strolls through the empty rooms with tremendously high ceilings that hasn't been this peaceful since the day her baby first came home in her arms, but as she makes her way down the hall toward his room, her chest again feels heavy.

Brian claimed he needed privacy and forbade his parents from entering his room. Even the housekeeper hardly crossed the threshold, and the air inside is stale. Surprisingly, Leslie doesn't wait for her to arrive. She opens the blinds and strips the bed herself. Dirty dishes and empty water bottles scatter the floor, along with drug paraphernalia unfamiliar to her. The house belongs to Leslie and her husband, who should have set boundaries. She now wishes things had been different.

She disrupts the mess, tossing everything into the hallway, wiping down the furniture, and pulling fresh bedding from the closet. Each motion feels like therapy to rid herself of the disappointment in her son and herself as a parent. Still wearing her pajamas, she gathers the trash and bedding together and stuffs it into the garbage can outside, along with her guilt.

There is no longer any sign of Brian living there, and she prays the boarding school will keep him long-term. After a long hot shower, she dresses and begins her day with a renewed sense of calm.

Brian has no idea what time it is when he finally reaches the facility, but the air is chilly and the sun is high in the clear blue sky. The men that accompanied him on the plane stand on either side of him in a small vestibule past the entrance, barely speaking throughout the entire ordeal. The drugs he took hours before while partying with friends have lost any effect, and his body craves more.

A soft-spoken man with salt and pepper hair greets Brian and leads him through a door to a desk in his office.

"After detox, you can join the other boys in the program."

"How long will I be here?"

"That's entirely up to you. Each student starts with the bare minimum. You will earn back privileges as you progress in the program."

A counselor who looks like he may have been a boarding school student at one time shows Brian to his room down a sterile hallway to a metal door painted the same color as the walls. It squeaks open. The space is empty and cold with only hard surfaces: a bare floor, shiny white walls separated by black plastic baseboards, and a twin-sized bed with a thin mattress next to a nightstand with a single drawer.

"There is a journal on the nightstand. An entry every day is mandatory," the counselor says as he shuts the door.

"Fuck that!" Brian says under his breath.

When the caller ID shows the facility's name a few weeks later, just when Leslie is starting to adjust to her son away, her first instinct is to ignore it. On the fourth ring, she finally answers with a tingling heat on her chest and hives developing that look like mosquito bites.

"Mom?"

"Hi, Brian. How are you?"

"Mom, you have to get me the fuck out of here!"

"Brian, please understand. We love you and want what is best for you."

"I'm not staying here!"

Someone takes the phone away from him, and his mother can hear the usual tantrum in the background that her son displays when he doesn't get his way.

"Mrs. Simmons?"

"Yes. What happened?

"Don't worry. Brian is taking longer than most, but he will eventually conform."

"Now what?"

"He will need to earn another call."

Leslie hangs up the phone, her whole body trembling.

Several months later, Brain finally hit a small milestone, and his parents imagine the program may have been the answer all along and fly to Utah to see him. The visit includes a tour of the grounds and a ceremony. Then the Simmons have permission to take their son off property for a few hours.

They check into a five-star hotel, get up early, and drive a rented SUV to the boarding school. Leslie plans a celebratory dinner for the three of them in the evening. Then it's off to catch a flight bound for Paris for a much-needed getaway.

After months apart, the parents almost forget their previous discrepancies until they lay eyes on their son. The tears Leslie cries are not happy ones as she had hoped they would be. Brian's anger has not subsided since the night they ripped him from his bed like a newborn from the womb. As they walk out of the building together, he casts the hand his mother tries to place in his away.

The little family the adoption agency brought together years ago now drives downtown in silence. How did the caseworker feel when she handed the newborn baby over to them, creating a family unit as if she were God himself? Was the caseworker responsible for the failure of this union? And did Leslie wish she had waited for the baby girl she thought she wanted instead, or would that situation have been worse?

When the vehicle stops in front of the restaurant, Brian unlocks the back door and escapes down an alley.

"Run after him," Leslie screams, but trying to catch him on foot is useless. There is no way he can outrun his son, so Mr. Simmons circles the block several times until he spots him down a narrow path between two tall buildings. A young man wearing a knit beanie rides a battered bicycle on the sidewalk not far from the SUV, and Mr. Simmons waves him over with a hundred-dollar bill.

"Want to make a hundred bucks?"

"For what?"

He shows the man a photo on his phone.

"I need you to find my son and bring him back here. He ran through there on the other side of that building," he says, pointing.

The man snatches the hundred and rides away. Several minutes pass before it's evident he isn't coming back.

"Call the school," Leslie says.

"We can't. Our son is in our possession for an hour, and now he's gone?"

They drive around until they come to a block with bars and strip clubs and enter a crowded parking lot filled with potholes as the sun dips behind the clouds. The attendant that day, a tall man about the same age as Mr. Simmons, notices something is wrong.

"You're not from around here, are you?"

"No. We are looking for our son," Mr. Simmons says, holding up his phone.

"I saw him earlier."

"Are you sure?"

"Positive. Your boy went into that building."

"Let's go," Leslie says.

"You can't go in there, ma'am. It's a drug house." Mr. Simmons draws a breath and turns to his wife. "Stay here, Leslie. I'm going to get him."

Out of desperation, Leslie strikes up a conversation with the attendant. He is not the type she usually associates with but she learns he also has a son addicted to drugs. It is a club that all parents fear, no matter their social status, and no parent wants to belong to. Brian is high as a kite and curled up on the floor when his father finds him.

The difference between having money and not is the options money gives you. The parking attendant doesn't have access to a treatment program for his son, but Leslie and her husband do. They summon the school's administrator and board the plane to Paris with Brian safely back in treatment. Brian's body was the only thing he could trade for drugs that night without a penny to his name. It is something they never discuss and try to forget.

Leslie calls Gayle to rehash the visit.

"How could you let your husband go into a house like that?"

"What were we supposed to do?" Leslie asks defensively. "What would you have done?"

"Don't ask me. I don't know from that."

"It was like something out of a movie, and I swear I will never let Brian put us in danger again."

Unfortunately, while helpful for minors, these boarding schools cannot keep an eighteen-year-old against their will, and eventually their son's time runs out.

The counselors assure the Simmons that Brian has turned a corner in therapy upon his release. With support from his parents and coping skills under his belt, he has every opportunity to prove himself and does appear calmer than ever. Before long, he's on his way, taking one college course online and working part-time as an optician's assistant.

An air about him wins the staff of girls in the doctor's office over immediately. The clothes Leslie buys him are expensive, his slight build lends itself to them, and he quickly learns how to manipulate people with his good looks. Besides pulling charts and walking patients to the exam rooms, he orders lunches and empties the garbage while the girls answer the phones.

A position opens up selling eyewear, and the doctor offers it to Brian. The job of hand-selecting dozens of designer frames and sunglasses for patients to try on is tedious but one of the most important. The profit on frames and lenses is enough to pay much of the overhead in the office. After an exam, patients have to pass the display of glasses to check out, and none can resist the charm of Brian, who takes one look at the shape of their faces and can guess which ones will flatter them. Patients begin to ask for him by name. Mr. Simmons, waiting for an opportunity like this to praise him, takes Brian for his driver's license and then leases him a BMW.

Things are looking up until Leslie comes downstairs early one morning and notices her purse on the dining room table. It's odd. She always hides it in the side cabinet of the buffet. There are a few loose bills in her wallet, and she can't remember how much she had in there previously. It doesn't make sense that Brian would steal. He receives a hefty paycheck and shouldn't need the money.

The sun hasn't risen yet when Leslie's housekeeper texts for the third day in a row claiming her daughter has the flu. For several months now, she has had only one cleaning girl, and this one takes complete advantage.

The dry cleaning is in the second bedroom, where the delivery service left it. If it isn't put away, Mr. Simmons will start to complain. In the dark, Leslie walks through the living room to get it and notices streaks in the glass that cause her to stop and examine them. Then she freezes. There is a man in her backyard walking toward the house. When he gets closer, she sees it's Trevor, Brian's friend from high school, with a massive spider tattoo on his neck. Why would someone get a tattoo like that? And what is he doing here?

Trevor walks straight to the back of the house, where her son lets him in through the cabana bath. Leslie doesn't confront them but instead calls the security gate and instructs them not to allow Brian any visitors.

The next day Leslie's son doesn't show up at work. No one at the office knows of his past, only that he drives a BMW and lives with his parents in an expensive neighborhood nearby. The next day, he looks disheveled but explains his absence by saying he slept through his alarm after a night of food poisoning.

And a few days later, his car goes missing.

"Cars don't just disappear," his father says. But it is never found.

All the signs point to their son returning to drug use, but Leslie and her husband continue to make excuses for him until he loses the job.

"Have you seen the order for Mrs. Horowitz?" the optician's assistant asks.

"We should have received them last week in the order Brian placed," the manager says, looking up from her computer screen.

The staff searches the office for the package containing several thousands of dollars in designer frames but can't locate it.

The doctor hears them and checks the security footage. The camera, recently installed, caught Brain carrying the missing box out the back door.

That evening two uniformed police officers appear at the house.

"Good evening, ma'am. We are looking for Brian Simmons. Is he your son?"

"Yes. What is this about?"

"Is he at home? We need to speak to him."

Leslie leads the police through the expansive rooms. Except for the static on the police radios, it is quiet when the officers knock on his bedroom door.

After some rustling inside, the door finally opens, and an officer steps forward.

"We are here to collect the package you stole from your employer."

"What package?"

"Don't try to deny it, son. He has you on camera."

Brian slides the cardboard box from under his bed, and the police place him under arrest.

Parents will spend their last dollar if they think it would save their child from harm and themselves from embarrassment. Leslie and her husband used their retirement savings on the treatment program and still hire an attorney to attempt to have the charges dropped.

Then one night, while Brian is out, there is a burglary.

Leslie's slender ankles and wrists are tied to a chair with rope in her living room. She can barely move them without the friction of the rope digging further into her delicate skin. Her husband, next to her, is also bound to his chair.

They watch as two men in ski masks ransack their home. It is hard for Leslie to breathe with the scratchy bandana covering her mouth. The beat of her heart pounds so hard she can hear it inside her head as the men pass her several times in the semi-dark living room. Her biggest fear is rape, and she prays they aren't here for that.

The taller of the two men walk toward the hidden safe in the bookcase. It contains the couple's cash and jewelry. No one knows about the safe and its contents except for Brian.

As they rip the safe from the wall, Leslie notices the spider tattoo on the one closest to her, and her fear turns to fury.

Mr. Simmons turns his chair on its side and wriggles out of the restraints after the two men leave. He frees his wife and grabs his phone.

"Call the police! Brian had something to do with this," Leslie says.

"I can't call the police on my son," he replies, and with that, she grabs the phone herself and dials 911.

CHAPTER NINE:

Jill Fontaine

ONE LAZY MORNING BEFORE MY FIRST CLIENT, I PLACE my supplies on my desk and look at the schedule taped to my lamp, indicating the day ahead. There are no surprises, no names I don't recognize; every client is familiar, and I know what to expect from each one. Some days are like visiting friends, fun and carefree.

Today is not one of those days.

10:00 - Brenda (never passes the coffee station without taking a bagel). The cream cheese remains under her nails as I work, and she will leave before Marcia arrives if possible because she can't stand the sound of her voice.

11:00 - Marcia (loud and imposing) entertains me with details of her daughter's upcoming wedding plans but lets me pick her polish color, a definite plus.

:king at her cuticles). She

.en she finally arrives, she
start.

ʌ piece of jewelry or a Chanel

.er ailments while I simultane-
er conversation nearby to distract

.s don't call, and she doesn't know
why). I could .

5:00 - Trisha (se.. .later, always has a story).

6:00 - Jill (lost a child).

Some stories in the salon come home with me like an over-
coat I can't take off. I even dream about them. Jill's story is one I
will never forget.

She gets the urge to spring-clean early on a Saturday, strip-
ping beds and separating laundry into piles, when her husband
informs her that his sister is having a birthday celebration in
the afternoon.

He likely knew about the swim party for his niece days
before and forgot to mention it, never considering the preparation
for an outing like this. Jill has a gift card she can repurpose, and
the boys have new bathing suits, but the last thing she wants to do
is stop what she's doing and get three boys dressed to go.

"You can stay," her husband says, noticing her angst. They
act as a team, always willing to make life easier for the other.

"You want to take all three of them by yourself, even the
baby?" Jill asks.

"Of course," he says. "My mom will be there."

The thought of having a few hours to herself and deep-clean-
ing the house without interruption sounds like heaven.

She packs sunscreen, towels, swim trunks, and enough bottles and diapers for the day. Before zipping up the bag, Jill ensures the baby's pacifier is inside. Otherwise, he may not nap for her husband.

Standing in the driveway in her bare feet, she waves goodbye with her entire family in her minivan, each of the boys strapped safely inside. Alex, the middle child, is smiling and holding his favorite toy dinosaur in his hands.

Jill is not a stay-at-home mom. She works as a secretary all week, then comes home to start dinner and feed the family before her husband leaves to work the night shift. Opposite work schedules solve the babysitting issue. Someone is always around to care for the new baby, who recently turned one, but the housework piles up during the week, and nothing gets done if it isn't pressing.

The boys' rooms desperately need vacuuming. She can only imagine what has accumulated under the beds. And dozens of shorts, t-shirts, and pajamas must be folded and put away. Maybe today it will finally happen.

Jill pulls her long wavy brown hair up in a ponytail on top of her head and prepares the brisket she's making for dinner. It will need to sit in the oven on low heat for the entire day to come out fork-tender. Meanwhile, she picks up toys and wipes down baseboards before vacuuming.

Cleaning can be like meditation. The repetitive motion doesn't require thought, opening the mind to run wild. A song from her portable speaker sparks her memory, and she's thinking about her high school days when the phone rings. Stopping would break her momentum and take too much precious time. The third time it rings, though, she answers. She can see from the caller ID it is her husband, and her heart sinks.

"What's wrong?"

His voice sounds muffled and far away.

"Take my car and meet me at Memorial Hospital."

"What? Who's in the hospital?"

"It's Alex."

She prays that he needs stitches, but something tells her it's much worse.

Later there is no memory of turning off the oven, slipping into the pair of flip-flops discarded yesterday by the door, or getting herself into the car. Jill's body trembles as she drives to where her son lies waiting.

Her husband is with his sister outside the sliding doors of the emergency entrance. They should be with Alex, who has never been to the hospital and is probably frightened. Jill leaves the car in the roadway and runs to them.

"Why are you out here?"

They attempt to explain—each taking over when the other can't speak.

The pool was full of kids splashing about when Jill's husband arrived with the boys in tow. Once they changed into their swim trunks, the oldest sat on a raft while Alex, the three-year-old, stood on the second step playing with the little army men he found in the water.

Alex standing in the pool on the steps was nothing new. He couldn't swim but never left his spot on the steps any other time. Jill's husband left for the store when his sister said they needed ice.

One of the army men was floating just out of Alex's reach a few minutes later. He leaned forward to grab it and lost his balance. His grandmother had the baby, showing him off to the other partygoers with her back turned. The pool was cloudy, full of splashing screaming kids, and by the time the grandmother turned back around, Alex was on the bottom.

When Jill's husband returned from the store with the bags of ice, he saw the ambulance parked in front of his sister's house with the lights flashing. He ran to the backyard, where a paramedic worked on Alex's lifeless body. It wasn't until they reached the hospital that a doctor delivered the news that Jill's middle son, Alex, could not be revived.

Her knees give out on the sidewalk in front of the emergency entrance, and she sobs on the ground. Her husband picks her up under her arms and helps her to a bench. How could this happen? Why did she let him take her babies to the party without her?

She pictures her son's deep-set brown eyes. Was he waiting for his mommy to save him as darkness overcame him? Hopefully, he didn't suffer.

The guilt everyone involved in this preventable death feels is immense. Although no one expected Jill's older son to watch his brother, he was in the pool when it happened, not paying attention. Jill's husband will never forgive himself for leaving to go to the store, and the grandmother blames Jill for not being there.

Everyone grieves differently. Jill finds comfort at the cemetery, sitting on the grass near the resting spot where her son's body lies, whereas her husband never returned there after the funeral. Neither will ever be truly happy again. They smile and even laugh sometimes but blissfully happy, the feeling before the accident when they took every blessing they had for granted? That they will never be again.

People keep saying it will get better, but how can it? Everything is a reminder. If Alex had his own room, it might stay as it was, the bedsheets never washed and the clothes still in the closet. But their oldest son sleeps in the bedroom alone now, and is it fair to shove the memory of the little brother he lost in his face? The grieving mother forces herself to pack three cardboard boxes of Alex's belongings and places them in the attic for safekeeping.

Returning to the car wash she frequented before the accident feels strange. Nothing is as it was before. The attendant takes her keys, and she enters the building. Through the walls come the sounds of the water spraying and then the hum of the warm air evaporating the droplets left behind. She silently prays she will never forget the features on her son's tiny face.

When the van is ready, she walks outside and tips the attendant, and he gives her the toy dinosaur Alex held the last time she saw him alive that must have fallen under the seat. Jill places it on the entry table when she gets home, and it remains there for years as a constant reminder.

How did mothers send their boys to fight for our country in wartime, knowing they may never return? Every mother is fortunate if they never know such agony.

When Jill's pain is no longer a fresh wound, she still struggles with the loss. Sitting in the wake of my clients' emotions is difficult. They feel better after they pour their hearts out, but often their intense energy steals every ounce of mine.

Thankfully, Trisha stays after her nails are dry to talk to Jill. Trisha takes our minds off anything serious. She doesn't work and lives off of the settlement from her last divorce. It is frivolous for her to buy a costly gym membership, but she does anyway and keeps track of what she eats on an app. It's a fallacy that you have to spend money to lose weight. Even home gym equipment like a treadmill or a stationary bike promising to give you a taste of the outdoors is unnecessary. Open up the front door. Beyond it is grass and sky and smells not duplicated on the screen of the gym equipment. No video of Europe or Alaska can measure up to walking through a morning fog as the sun rises, no matter where you live.

Clients learn from each other, so I stay quiet and let them talk. One will help another tremendously in passing without realizing it, and I try not to stand in the way.

"I just wish I knew that he is all right," Jill says.

"Have you ever seen a medium?" Trisha asks. "I know one in Miami who is worth the drive."

On what would have been Alex's sixteenth birthday, Jill goes to see the medium on Trisha's recommendation, hoping to connect with the boy she lost so long ago. If only we all had a crystal ball or a person with special powers to guide us, life would be so simple to figure out.

On the way, she tries to picture a sixteen-year-old Alex and finds it impossible. He will always be three. Jill left early for the appointment but arrives at the small Florida-style home in Miami a few minutes late. An accident on the highway held up traffic.

Religious paraphernalia adornes the concrete front steps, and she is nervous, but there is no turning back now. The medium was expecting her, and she likely heard the car drive up no matter where she was inside the tiny house shaped like a box. The walls are stucco, the low roof is barrel-tiled, and the whole thing would probably fit inside Jill's living room.

The medium, short with a round face, answers the door in a black maxi dress with long sleeves and leads Jill into a small room with a chandelier probably meant for formal dining. Only a strip of sunlight scattered with dust runs across the space between the heavy curtains and the table. Before Jill's eyes completely adjust to the darkness, she finds the velvet chair the medium motions for her to sit on.

The woman closes the curtain and lights a candle. The effect is that of a séance. One would imagine the dead would need a space like this to appear.

"Did you bring me an article from the deceased?"

Jill reaches down and pulls the toy dinosaur she grabbed at the last minute out of her purse. The woman holds it in her hands and closes her eyes. They sit for a long time in silence.

"This baby who passed away was your first child?"

"Second."

"A boy?"

"Yes."

Anyone could have figured that much out from the toy.

"It was a long time ago?"

"Yes."

"His name began with an A?"

"Yes, Alex."

She's getting more specific. Jill is impressed.

"Alex says he knows you keep his memory by the front door."

Jill's breath catches in her throat. There is no way this woman could have known that the toy sat there all these years.

"He knows that you visit the cemetery often. He says he's with you when you are there."

"Tell him I can feel him," Jill says between sobs.

"Your grandfather on your mother's side is with him."

"I never met my grandfather."

"He is very proud of you."

"I should have never let my boys go to the party without me. Alex would still be here."

"Children are a gift, and not everyone is meant to live a long life," the woman says.

"I need to know if he is all right."

"Go ahead and speak to him. He is listening."

The sun seems to be in a different location in the sky when Jill leaves, but the digital clock in the car confirms it has only been an hour.

Did she witness an actual spiritual meeting or someone who preys on others' sorrow for financial gain? We may never know but we find comfort where we can, and Jill needed it desperately.

CHAPTER TEN:

Courtney Wilmington

MY OLDEST AND SWEETEST CLIENT, JUDY, WELCOMES me from my desk when I walk through the door.

"Take your time. I'm early," she says.

She tells me about one of her sons as I remove her polish. I have heard the story before, but I never let on. The longer she talks, the less chance she will fall asleep during the appointment.

I don't mind an incoherent client, allowing me to work faster without entertaining. But half the time Judy falls into a deep sleep during the second half of her appointment. Polishing the whites of her French manicure can be a real challenge when her fingers start to curl inward.

My next client, Courtney Wilmington, is an attractive young attorney who rarely leaves the office early enough to have her nails done after work, so I usually see her during her lunch break.

She has two children she adores, primarily raised by her husband, who doesn't work outside the home. She pays the bills, and Ricky chauffeurs the kids, shops for groceries, and plans dinners. The reverse in roles was never a problem until Courtney started comparing her life to Danielle's.

I also do Danielle's nails.

The two met in Lamaze class toward the end of their first pregnancies, and now the babies are in third grade together. Danielle is striking with dark hair and a slim figure, and her husband is a successful realtor, mostly selling mansions on the east side of town. Danielle adores her husband, and he loves his wife. All she has to do is ask, and he will try his best to make all her dreams come true.

Danielle wants everything that Courtney has. So while they could have afforded a more expensive house, Danielle chose a house only a few blocks from her friend.

The original owners lived in the house for less than a year, but Danielle guts it and upgrades the finishes anyway. Most of the neighbors are young, with small children, and have little extra money to spend so readily, yet it doesn't stop Danielle from posting photos of the renovation progress. It is fun to see someone enjoy their life so much. Still, when she starts posting every gift her husband brings home to her on social media, some girls feel their marriages lack the excitement hers has.

Courtney is not interested in competing with her friends. When Danielle picks the same minivan she and Ricky have, the same color even, she is annoyed. "She's a stalker," Courtney says during her nail appointment. "The other moms at school ask if we are related because she's dressing like me." I try to diffuse the situation.

"Imitation is the sincerest form of flattery."

The loaded luxury minivans with automatic sliding doors are popular for families with small children in this quiet suburban town. Dozens of them in every color snake the elementary school parking lot long before dismissal. While they wait for their children, the moms gather around Ricky to chat. "I heard you're getting new neighbors," one dressed in sweatpants and a baseball cap says to Courtney's husband.

"Yes, they're from Ohio. I think it's a job transfer," Ricky says.

"Aren't they the third family to live in that house?"

"Yes."

"Well, I hope they stay."

On the day the new family moves in, Courtney and Ricky are outside. They see the husband first, a wormy little guy in shorts and a shirt that makes him look slightly prepubescent, and then out from the garage stacked with boxes comes the mismatched wife.

The pretty blonde could have come off a beach in California rather than a small town in Ohio. "We live right across the street if you need anything," Courtney says, pointing toward her house.

"Thank you. I'm Julia, and this is Sergio."

"Do you guys have any children?"

"We have a boy and a girl."

"Same."

Julia takes Courtney up on the offer to be of help and asks for recommendations for local eateries. Courtney emails her a list of her favorites and includes must-see places to take the kids, and in return Julia makes a tray of lasagna on Saturday and brings it over. "We won't have it without you," Courtney says. "Go get Sergio and the kids, and we can have drinks by the pool before dinner."

It only takes a few minutes for Ricky to straighten up the downstairs and wipe down the kitchen counters while his wife locates a bottle of Pinot Noir and four stemless glasses.

We should all take a lesson from the little ones. As the two new playmates come through the door, looking surprisingly like their father, Courtney's kids run toward them. The new kids also have clothing that appears too tight and hairstyles different from their own, but children don't judge that sort of thing. They only want to play.

It would be nice to keep this new friendship between the two families quiet and not include Danielle. Still, privacy is an issue in a development where the houses sit so close together, and avoiding someone is almost impossible.

"Courtney doesn't return my calls," Danielle complains to me.

"She works a lot. She's probably just busy."

"She has time for Julia; they are always together."

"Well, it's convenient; they are right across the street, aren't they?"

"Yes. I should have bought a house on that block." Changing the subject, she says, "I'm thinking of getting a puppy."

"Really? What kind?"

"A Maltese."

"Doesn't Courtney have a Maltese?"

"Yes, they are the best dogs."

The Instagram post announcing the new pet's arrival doesn't sit well with Courtney. Danielle and her husband are holding hands in the picture, and the hand-holding is more bothersome than the breed of the dog. Ricky never tries to touch her anymore. Another problem with social media. Everyone's marriage seems happier, and it feels like they are taking the opportunity to rub it in.

Danielle has no idea her posts are offensive to others, even after several moms unfollowed her. She is too busy scheming a way to get back in Courtney's good graces and, at the same time, introduce herself to the new couple.

From the window of her office upstairs, Courtney sees Danielle's minivan pass by. She spends more time driving through the neighborhood than anyone else, constantly dropping off and picking up the kids. It's likely to see what everyone else is doing.

A few minutes later, Danielle passes by again, stopping directly in front of the window. Ricky and the kids are at soccer practice, so Courtney has to stop preparing for the upcoming trial she is working on and answer the door.

The kids' backpacks and shoes litter the stairs. Nothing is ever out of place at Danielle's, so Courtney strategically opens the front door just enough to slip out, concealing the foyer's disarray. She wishes Ricky was better at making the kids pick up their things.

Danielle has a stack of flyers in her hand, and she hands one to Courtney.

"What's this?"

"I'm hosting a party with a bounce house for the kids to celebrate the end of the school year."

"Nice. Who else did you invite?"

"Just a few other couples and their kids."

"Did you ask Julia and Sergio?"

"Yes, and two families from my block."

Just then, Courtney's phone rings. "I must take this call, but we will be there." She refuses to let Danielle hang out with Julia without her.

"Great," Danielle says, but the front door is already closed.

On the day of the party, Courtney pulls the invitation off the refrigerator. The party theme is a luau, and the attire is casual. She chooses a strapless midi dress from her closet, perfect for hiding the extra ten pounds she can't lose since her last pregnancy.

The party house is awash with rainbow-colored leis that Danielle's children hand out at the front door to all the guests as they walk in, and she's wearing a caftan and flats, looking like the perfect hostess. When Julia arrives in a tight pair of jean shorts from the Gap, some of the dads, seeing her for the first time, fail the attempt to hide their stares.

Sergio makes his way to the backyard in a pink lei, unaware that it does zero for his masculinity. There are speakers shaped like decorative rocks in the corners of the swimming pool, with Eighties dance music emanating from them.

Danielle's husband pours a glass of eighteen-year scotch for his guest and returns to the grill to finish cooking the steaks. Sergio follows.

"Did this pool come with the house?"

"There was a small pool, but my wife redesigned it."

"That had to be expensive."

"It was, but you know what they say, happy wife, happy life."

Inside, Danielle has prepared a buffet table ahead of time, not wanting to miss a second of the action at her party. A tall mom with red hair always in everyone's business seeks out Julia.

"I heard your son is in the gifted program with my son."

"Yes, he loves the teacher."

"I told the principal if my son didn't qualify for gifted, I would pull him out and send him to private. I didn't want him held back in the mainstream class."

"My daughter is in a mainstream class."

"That's too bad."

Julia turns to Courtney, "How rude. What kind of people live around here?"

"Ohio must be a different world," Courtney says.

The drinks lighten the mood, and the girls dance the night away on a makeshift dance floor in the family room. The kids are embarrassed by their moms and retreat upstairs. Courtney and Julia end up outside with Danielle by night's end, sprawled out on lounge chairs.

"When do you leave for vacation?" Danielle asks.

"Next week if I can wrap things up at work," Courtney says.

Julia looked surprised. "Where are you going?"

"We take a summer trip to California for a few weeks to visit Ricky's family. The kids love it there."

"I can imagine."

Danielle declares victory to herself, knowing Courtney's history better than Julia. She has many pictures with Courtney on her phone from the party and gives herself a pat on the back in the morning when she has a record number of likes on her posts. Julia is tagged and starts following the hostess @lifeofaprincess.

When Courtney and her family leave for California, Danielle strategically passes their block on her way home from carpool and notices Julia unloading groceries from her car.

"Hi Julia, do you have time for coffee at my house?"

"Sure, let me finish bringing these bags in."

Danielle parks and grabs the last two bags for an excuse to walk into the house. You can tell a lot about a person by how they live. Julia has no idea she is under a microscope.

"When did you guys buy this house?" Danielle asks.

"We didn't. It's a rental. Sergio's company transferred him with only a two-month notice, so there was no time to decide."

Danielle walks through the living room to check out the view in the back.

"Are you still waiting for your furniture to be delivered?"

"No. We sold it before moving here. I want to wait to see where we end up before I buy more."

"If you need a realtor, I'm sure my husband will make an exception for you. He usually deals in multi-million homes."

Julia unpacks the refrigerated food and leaves the rest on the counter. "Let's go," she says.

"Don't you want to finish putting things away?"

"I can do it later. Let's go out through the garage."

They step into the garage filled with unopened boxes.

"What is all this?"

"Oh, I haven't finished unpacking."

"If you haven't needed the stuff by now, you can probably get rid of it," Danielle suggests, cringing at the disorganization.

They ride the three blocks over in Danielle's van. The seats smell like a cross between laundry detergent and baby powder, and the scent surrounds Julia like aromatherapy.

"Your car is spotless. Court told me you keep everything immaculate." But the comment sounds nothing like a compliment.

Courtney calls then to ask Danielle to grab her mail while they are away. Danielle has her on speaker.

"Hey, Court."

Danielle has never called her Court before. It's odd.

"Hey," she says.

"Your ears must have been burning."

"Why? Who's there?"

"Julia. We were getting ready to have a cup of coffee. What's up?"

"I'm gone five minutes, and you are already with Julia?"

"Why is it a problem?"

"No, of course not," Courtney says, but then decides to ask her next-door neighbor to pick up the mail instead.

I do Courtney's nails after her vacation.

"How was it?" I ask.

"It was nice to be away, but the stalker started hanging out with Julia while we were gone. They've been shopping for furniture together."

"I heard."

"Has Danielle had her nails done?"

"Yes, last Thursday."

"What did she say?"

I have to be careful not to take sides in these situations or say anything that can come back to bite me.

"Haven't you seen her?"

"No, and I'm not planning to," Courtney says. For months, she avoids Danielle, and things are quiet.

Ricky is outside with one eye on his kids playing in the street and the other on his phone. Courtney texts to say she'll be late again, and he starts contemplating what to make for dinner.

Julia crosses the street toward him.

"What's up?"

"Hey," Ricky says.

Ricky can't help but notice how good Julia looks in running shorts.

Courtney doesn't exercise.

"Going for a run?" he asks.

"I wish. I am watching the kids ride their new bikes."

"I can keep an eye on them," Ricky says, "Or you can sit here?"

"I think I'll do that," she replies. Ricky stands up, grabs another chair out of the garage, and places it next to his. Danielle's van speeds by, passing the two, but she never takes her eyes off the road.

Ricky turns to Julia. "Your kids seem to like the bikes."

"Yes, I'm hoping they spend more time outside now that the weather is cooler."

"I know what you mean."

Something about the curve of Julia's mouth reminds Ricky of his girlfriend in high school. Funny, he hadn't noticed it before.

"So, how long have you been with Sergio?" he asks.

"Since high school. I was best friends with his sister."

"How convenient."

"Yes. It was."

"How about you? How long have you been with Courtney?"

"Ten years."

"Have you ever cheated on her?"

"You don't beat around the bush, do you?"

"Not really."

"Do I look like a cheater?"

"No, but you have a lot of time on your hands."

"So do you. Have you ever cheated?"

"Once. I was drunk at a party. That's why Sergio asked for the transfer to Florida. He went to high school with the guy," she says, giggling.

"How about a beer?" Ricky asks.

"Sure."

Julia follows Ricky inside.

He opens a bottle and pours it into two plastic cups.

"Cheers," he says, tapping his against hers.

"I like your sofa," she says, plopping down on one of the cushions, "I have been looking for a new one." Ricky doesn't say that his wife picked out the sofa, like everything else. The sectional smells like Courtney's perfume, but it doesn't deter what is about to happen. It isn't Ricky's fault. Men tend to have very little control by nature, and Julia is throwing herself at him.

He guzzles his portion of the beer and then sits on the edge of the coffee table, facing her. She moves forward, and their knees touch slightly, giving him the green light.

The first kiss, unexpected and passionate, will be a fantasy of his for years to come, and the running clothes she has on end up in a pile on the floor before either one gives their spouse a thought.

"I knew you were dangerous," he whispers in her ear.

Not even pretending to be modest, she dresses in the open while he anxiously grabs two water bottles from the fridge and says, "We better get back outside."

As soon as they reach the street, Julia's husband pulls into their driveway. Ricky awkwardly folds the chairs and takes them back inside the garage.

The kids ride up on the bikes, and Ricky calls out to his two, "Time to go in and get ready for dinner!"

Julia does the walk of shame back home to greet her husband. And her daughter appears. "We were looking for you, Mom. Where were you guys?"

"Just getting some water," Julia says, holding up her bottle.

Sergio tries to stay calm, but his instincts tell him something is off.

"You're hanging out with the stay-at-home dad?" he asks.

"No," she says, "it's not like that."

Her husband never says another word, but vows not to stand by while another loser tries to steal his precious wife. While Julia showers the next day, he installs a nanny cam pointed at the front door. It doesn't take long before Ricky shows up on the camera feed entering the house.

A loud slamming sound at dawn echoes outside and wakes Courtney the following Saturday. She remembers emails from work needing attention, and goes downstairs to the kitchen. Ricky heard the noise, too, because he is also up.

With a coffee cup in one hand and her laptop in the other, she looks out the front window and notices a moving van across the street stretching the length of the driveway. In pajama pants and a t-shirt, she slips into her Crocs and goes out the front door. Ricky doesn't follow.

The front door of Julia's house is open, and all the rooms are vacant save for a few empty boxes inside.

"They're gone," she says when she comes back in. "The movers said they left last night."

"Where did they go?" Ricky asks.

"I have no idea. I saw Julia yesterday. She didn't say anything."

"Who knows," Ricky says, tying his shoes. "They were kind of weird anyway."

"I thought you liked them."

"I'll be back in a little while. I'm going for a run."

The door closes behind him.

To leave in the middle of the night without telling anyone? What went on there?

Courtney pulls her phone from the charger in the kitchen. Lately, she keeps it downstairs at night so it won't disturb her sleep. There are several work-related messages and a text from an unknown number.

Just a heads up. Your husband is a scumbag

He seduced my wife while you were at work

I have plenty of proof if you don't believe me

In shock, Courtney goes upstairs, where the kids are still sleeping. She looks in on them, and tears roll down her face at the thought of her family separating.

All the nights she worked late in the office instead of coming to bed may have pushed him away. Naturally, he looked elsewhere for attention. It makes sense that he looked crushed when he left for his run. His girlfriend moved out in the night, probably without saying goodbye.

Now that they are gone, is it possible to ignore the texts and forget about the infidelity? Courtney deletes the messages and blocks the numbers from her contacts.

"What happened over there?" Danielle asks.

"We don't know."

"Strange, isn't it?"

"I guess you never know what's happening with some people."

"I guess not."

In the years that follow, Courtney uses a babysitter to watch her kids after school, so that her husband can finally work outside the home. She interviews several before choosing an older woman with a limp, and Danielle and Courtney become closer than ever.

CHAPTER ELEVEN:

The Pandemic

THE SALON IS BUSIER TODAY THAN IT'S BEEN IN months. I remove the KN95 mask covering my nose and mouth for the past eight hours straight. I am about to toss it into the garbage when my receptionist Lisa approaches me, heels clicking on the white marble floor, the phone one with the side of her head. She's on hold with whoever is on the line and says, "Kelly's client wants a manicure, and no one else is available." I've never been one to turn away business, and we lost so much during the pandemic that I'm inclined to stay and do her nails.

Kelly's client has dye, the color of shoe polish, smeared through her hair, the gel-like consistency slowly creeping down her forehead, extending the natural hairline. She doesn't look familiar, but it's hard to recognize people with a mask covering the entire lower half of their faces.

"Who usually does her nails?" I ask Lisa.

"I think she goes to the Vietnamese, but she's afraid now."

"Of the virus?"

"Yes."

Could it be true? Will the virus that originated in China be the demise of the Asian walk-in nail salons and the start of clients lining up again for acrylic sets like we did in the Eighties?

I'm not sure I could keep up that pace anymore.

I have always been obsessed with nails. In high school, when acrylics were all the rage, a part-time job in a small boutique in the mall funded my addiction. My heart skipped a beat whenever I pushed through the glass doors of Future Nails, one of the first nail-only salons in South Florida.

The mirrored walls gave the illusion of double the number of women inside but still did not compare to the ten thousand square foot full-service salons I work in later. At Future Nails, table after table of black-clad nail technicians, not much older than I was, filed and buffed inch-long false nails into perfection, and the customers were mesmerized, unable to stop staring at their hands. I knew the feeling. I had been there before.

After checking in at the front desk, the receptionist whisked me away to a nail station where a girl with long dark hair and bright pink daggers took my hands in hers.

"Active length?"

"A little shorter than yours, please."

"Square or round?"

"Square."

"What color?" I looked through the assortment on her desk.

"This red is pretty."

I went to school the next day wearing a purple acid-washed mini skirt with black kitten heels, sporting the fifty-dollar red nails. The bright color and the sound of them tapping my desk got plenty of attention from friends in my second-hour class, but

Ms. Ellington didn't appreciate the distraction. The nails didn't violate any rules in the Student Handbook, but my skirt did not quite reach the fingertip length requirement, and she used it as an excuse to send me straight to the principal's office.

Had it been another day, not the mid-term exam, and had my grades not already teetered on failure in that class, I would have slid past this little blunder, and it wouldn't have ruined my GPA. But this was the day I switched gears in my junior year, and as my friends prepared to take the SAT, I began a forty-year career in the fast-paced creative vocation of Nail Extension Specialist.

My parents, less than thrilled at my decision, pressured me to at least enroll in a few classes at community college, hoping I would earn a degree and get a real job. So I studied for a while, but college isn't for everyone. I preferred the salon where we dressed in the latest fashions, transformed short peeling nails into long talons, polished to perfection, and where clients praised me for my skills and vowed never to let anyone else touch their hands.

At the end of the long workday, I collected my tips, high on the adrenaline of doing something well and getting proper compensation or high on the acrylic fumes. I wondered what other job could have as much gratification.

We used a dental acrylic monomer on our customers' nails long after reports of dermatitis and damage to the nail plate caused the FDA to ban its use in salons. The rubber cement consistency went on like butter, hardened to concrete, and could completely transform a bitten natural nail into a vision. Acrylic was all we had back then, and nothing else was ever as secure or reliable. There were no odorless gel manicures, dip manicures, or tips that perfectly mimicked any length and shape. We had to use a form and build a nail from nothing. Natural-looking sculpted acrylic was an art that not everyone could perform well, especially as we did without a drill. Customers swarmed around the desk of the few who mastered it for the chance to sit with them, and everyone knew their name. As mine became well-known, the owner asked for a word with me.

"Ann sounds like a forty-year-old woman," she said.

"It does?"

"Yes. Let's call you Annie."

I never got used to it, and once it stuck, there was no going back.

Annie feels like a stage name, like the ones used by the nail techs at the Vietnamese salons. I'm sure Ashley and Kim were also made up and not names given to the girls by their Vietnamese parents, so we have that in common. Also, our ability to hustle.

Before the now popular walk-in nail salons appeared in South Florida in the early 2000s, saturating the market, American-born nail techs came in early, stayed late, and forfeited lunch and bathroom breaks to fit in as many appointments as possible. Those original customers became the bulk of my clientele, and that's how you make it in this business. Keep the customers you already have, and you never have to find new ones.

We feel the hit when the excess work slacks off, and I need to see what attracts so many women to the new-style salon.

When I arrive, it becomes clear. The salon welcomes customers without an appointment seven days a week, making it convenient for me to check them out on Sunday when fewer people are around. How would it look if anyone I knew saw me here?

The modestly dressed barely five-foot-tall receptionist, who speaks broken English, offers me a basic pedicure for twenty-seven dollars. The commission on an hour of service at that rate is less than minimum wage. How can these girls ever make money charging so little?

I have a bird's eye view of the entire room from the deluxe pedicure chair and let the built-in massage knuckles kneed my back while I peer around with my sunglasses covering my eyes like a spy. The nail technicians work meticulously. They have to get the same license from the state we do but train their employees in-house before they ever work on clients to use the same techniques and supplies until they are virtually interchangeable, so one doesn't offer something better than another. Then if an employee leaves, the client usually remains in the salon with another tech—a smart business move on their part.

While soaking my feet, I watch an entire row of girls robotically buff and polish nails in sync, their movements with the same ease and grace as a water ballet performance. The nail technicians stay on task, never speaking to the housewives whose husbands are home watching football or the women having a manicure before the next work week starts. And when the service is over, the clients move toward the door with hands in the air as if on cue. Then like clockwork, another round prances in.

I am aware of the upsell happening all around the room. I call it the "Would you like fries with that" method. My girl offers a paraffin treatment and a reflexology massage for only a few dollars more on top of the price for the basic pedicure. Who would say no? It was brilliant.

In our salon, if the busy receptionist asks the fourteen nail techs if anyone can squeeze in a nail repair, they all have an excuse why they can't. The reasons range from "I'm leaving for the day" or "My next client will be here in five minutes" to "I have my period." So we lose those customers to the competition when we push them out the door to find another salon that will accommodate them.

I get it. No one wants to do the dreaded nail repair, but it's poor customer service not to guarantee the work. And why can't the girls see it's a potential new client handed to them on a silver platter? When a client is happy with one nail, it can lead to a booking for a complete service. It happens all the time.

As the hot towels warm my legs, I watch a tech named Toni Lee squeeze in a walk-in nail repair while her next customer lingers in the front, happy to relax and check her emails on her phone before her appointment.

Toni Lee makes a sour face when the repair client sits down and says, "You want me to wax eyebrow?"

I watch intently. Toni Lee can't possibly take the time for another service while her next client is waiting only a few feet away. But in one quick motion, she stands up, flips the client's head back, smears a popsicle stick full of hot wax from a nearby rolling tray on her face, and rips it off, adding eighteen dollars to her bill plus tip, all while the one with the appointment has her head down. That's what it means to hustle.

Twenty minutes have passed since I arrived, my girl is already polishing my toes, and I hear someone say, "ANNIE! WHAT ARE YOU DOING HERE?"

I panic and look to see who is potentially exposing my undercover investigation. It's Vanessa, a former client of ours.

"Having a pedicure," I say in response, pointing to my feet.

"Oh, I thought you would do that at your salon?"

"No, our girls are much too busy," I offer, then stop, thinking it best not to overexplain.

"I love having my services done on Sundays, don't you?"

"Yes," I say, the pits of my underarms profusely sweating, but nobody else is paying us any mind.

As Vanessa sits for her manicure, two customers begin to cause a scene at the entrance. The owner shows up from the back room with the presence of a Gestapo.

"You don't like? Then you leave!" she spits. I am shocked that clients like Vanessa bow down to this tyrant. It is a side of them I've never seen. Our clients expect us to cater to them. And we do because, after all, the customer is always right.

There will always be difficult personalities, but you're not marrying them, just doing their nails. Think about how much a client pays for their service? How much does that add up to over a month? A year? A lifetime? If you want to succeed in this business, never turn away a client with a pulse when there is still room in your schedule.

My girl leaves me to dry and moves to the next chair, prepping for her fifth pedicure of the morning. I hand her a sizeable tip, pay my bill, and slide out, my toenails perfectly polished and my heels soft from the paraffin. The Vietnamese have us beat in time management and consistency. The only thing I could see that we have over them is the close relationships we've built over the years. It is the only thing they are unable to improve upon or duplicate. But it comes with a tremendous amount of responsibility.

The seventeen-year-old me, enlightened and corrupted by what I heard, didn't know how much knowledge would come from the women whose nails I did, treating me the exact opposite of Ms. Ellington. They complimented my clothes and jewelry and wanted the same color polish I wore. They showered me with gifts, set me up on dates with their sons, and trusted me with their deepest, darkest secrets. Many were my mentors without even knowing it. To learn, all we ever have to do is listen.

Several of my nail tech friends threw away the file to raise children as stay-at-home moms, but I stayed put, raising my children and working simultaneously. Most of the advice I received from the older moms with more experience was helpful and far outweighed the hurtful unsolicited kind I endured over the years. I took the good with the bad. The nasty and unscrupulous had maybe even more to share, teaching me what not to do in any given situation.

I made the mistake of mentioning to my client, Leslie, that we allowed our son, a drummer in an alternative rock band, to play in clubs underage. Very underage, like ten. There was a photo of the band on my desk.

"We are with him at all times."

"Still, how can he go to school the next day without a good night's sleep?"

"He always manages to wake up and get straight As."

"Are those tattoos on his arm real?"

"He's ten."

"I know, but I've seen your husband."

I didn't defend myself. It was my fault for displaying the picture and opening myself up to criticism. Again, this is business, not marriage or even a friendship. I smile and file. Saying nothing is so powerful. Like when customers ask whether my designer bag is authentic or my boobs are natural and how much I pay for my car each month. As time passed, I was more private with my own life, listening more and speaking less.

One morning at eleven fifteen, I was mid-stroke with my buffer, preparing Karen's nails for polish, when her crossbody bag started vibrating. She pulled her hand away to lift it, so I could extract her phone from the side compartment.

"Give me twenty minutes, and then meet me in the bus loop," she said as she stood up. "I have to go, Annie. Brad doesn't like the lunch they are serving at school today and wants me to bring him a drive-thru chicken sandwich."

"What about your nails?"

"Can I come back later for polish? He's waiting."

I admired the dedication, but was Karen helping him succeed? What will happen when he leaves for college? I waited and watched out of curiosity, and to my surprise, Brad thrived. He still dials his mother's number during her nail appointments with a question that can't wait. "Should I go to Chipotle for lunch or Panera?" But Brad graduated top of his class.

His mother, though, floundered without an identity of her own, and her marriage suffered for it. I saw Karen after a fight with her husband. They hadn't spoken in days.

"I'm ready for a truce," she said.

"Why don't you make his favorite dinner tonight?" I suggested. She hesitated and chuckled to herself. "I don't even know what his favorite dinner is."

Not every client bares their soul. Some prefer gossiping about their friends instead. These are the stories I live for, entertaining me while I work.

"You do Denise's nails?" Sheila asked after eyeing my schedule.

"Yes. For a while now."

"Did she tell you she cheated on her husband?"

"No." I make eye contact, encouraging more words.

"Please don't repeat this," she said, looking over her shoulder.

"Of course."

"The guy she cheated with was also married, but Denise thought surely he would leave his wife, and she started telling everyone that her husband liked to pee on her."

"Really?" I grimaced as much as my Botox would allow.

"Yes. And then, after the affair came out, the guy never ended up leaving, and Denise had to stay with her husband and back-pedal, correcting the story by saying it only happened once when they were drunk."

Note to self: write this one down for the book.

In late February 2020, with the first coronavirus cases all over the news and no idea what was coming, I began writing some of the most compelling stories I witnessed throughout my career. Most of us have a book inside of us, waiting to come out.

I have always been a passionate reader, from classic novels to self-help books, but the writing was challenging, having never written anything before. I thought about the scandals of cheating spouses, less-than-desirable in-laws, and significant financial problems. The tales I heard could compete with the best of the protagonists' stories in the books I read. Each one with a moral dilemma that teaches a valuable lesson. I needed to find a way to sort them all out if I were to share them with others.

I opened my mind and quietly wrote. Details long forgotten emerged and flowed effortlessly onto the paper, starting with my own story. I learned the craft of creative writing from a few dozen YouTube videos and then ran with it.

CHAPTER TWELVE:

Yours Truly

AT THIS POINT, I WORK BECAUSE I LOVE WHAT I DO and prefer a shorter client list, but I have no plans for tonight since we are still in pandemic mode, meaning my husband, Angelo, and I hardly leave the house, so I stay late to do Stacy's nails.

Before she sits, I wipe the chair and desk surface with an antibacterial solution and check my phone. There is a text from my mom. It's strange because we haven't spoken in over a year. I offer a shelf for Stacy's Chanel boy bag, so the acetone won't splash onto the caviar leather and ruin it. If I have to pay for Chanel, I at least want to enjoy it.

Looking down at her hands, I remember who this is. Names and faces I sometimes forget, but the hands I always recognize.

The middle finger on her left hand was closed in a car door when she was a little girl, and she lost the tip, so the nail grows down around the finger from the injury instead of coming straight out. I have to cut the damaged nail and finagle a false plastic tip on the end to mimic one like the other nine. This minor defect does not detract from Stacy's beauty, but resonates with me. Angelo, lost the same finger on the same hand in a police-involved shooting which in no way changes his appearance or demeanor. Our scars prove we have been through something and survived.

Stacy's phone vibrates with a news alert that she reads aloud. Working for so many hours, we are at the mercy of the client's memory to relay breaking news outside the salon bubble when they come in for an appointment. And lately, there are daily articles on the pandemic. "A person infected with Corona had dinner with eight family members. Six ended up in the hospital and later died."

I feel my chest tighten. I've never had anxiety before. It happens every time someone starts talking about the virus. Kelly walks over to check Stacy's hair color, and I try to take deep breaths behind the mask.

"When is the wedding?" Kelly asks.

"It was supposed to be next month, but we had to postpone it until October," Stacy says.

"How are the plans going?"

"There is a lot of drama."

"Isn't there always?" I say.

"I think we have more than usual. My daughter is marrying my husband's son."

Women react one of two ways when involved in a scandal like this. Either they don't mention it and hope no one knows, or like Stacy they lay it all out there and talk about themselves before anyone else has the opportunity.

"You can get shampooed," Kelly says.

I loosen my grip on Stacy's hand, and she walks to the shampoo bowl where Alex washes her hair.

"Wasn't she married to a dentist?" I ask Kelly.

"She was."

"What happened? She seemed so happy."

"They started hanging out with another couple who had season tickets to the Panther games. Stacy loves hockey, and the wife never really did, so she was happy to let Stacy take her place."

"And steal her husband?"

"I guess so. The two started bike riding on weekends, and the wife caught them together in her hot tub. Hang on. Stacy's coming back."

"Can you believe the bitch ex-wife didn't include us in the engagement party?" Stacy says to Kelly as she sits back down. "We have to have a separate party of our own."

"Were the kids always attracted to each other?" I ask.

"No, but it wasn't surprising. My husband's son is a clone of him, and my daughter is a clone of me. The wedding is the first time both families will be together in one place."

"You know I'm writing a book about my clients, right?" I say.

"You can use it," she says jokingly.

On the way home, I check to see if the grocery store has restocked toilet paper and order dinner on an app because most places still don't allow inside dining. But I need to call my mom back. Why am I so anxious?

It's not like I have to see her. It's only a phone call. She's safely tucked away in Mobile, Alabama, miles from South Florida and worlds away from Pandora's Box that opened when we met thirteen years ago, and the real-life fairy tale of Cinderella's mother returning to the castle to save her played out.

My birth mother, Diane, would have been just as happy not to meet the baby she abandoned at twenty-one, scared, alone, and unmarried. The mere sight of me as an adult filled her with the same guilt and shame she felt the rainy night at the hospital when she relinquished her rights for fear of tarnishing her reputation forever.

When my parents finally admitted they adopted me, I was an adult. I couldn't help but wonder if it's such a beautiful thing to adopt a child, why did it have to remain a secret? And once I knew, I pictured my biological mother pining away for me.

Children's Home Society of Miami, the agency that facilitated the adoption, mailed a letter to the last known address in an attempt to contact my birth mother on my behalf.

The letter made it as far as Diane's mother's house, to the nightstand in the guest room in a small stack of mail addressed to her, but Diane didn't see it until the following Christmas when she visited with her husband and three teenagers (my half-siblings).

The sunny seventy-degree day was light sweater weather for Floridians, but Diane and her family were ready for a day at the beach after the long drive from Illinois.

Diane's mother had dinner prepared when they returned, and the kids showered and dressed, hungry from frolicking in the ocean. The grandmother was a stickler for neatness, so while everyone enjoyed the salad, Diane threw laundry started earlier into the dryer to fold and put away later. But, upon separating the wet clothes, she noticed her husband's pen, left in a pocket, had exploded ink in streaks across her mother's new towels.

Familiar with her mother's wrath, if ever she was imperfect in any way, she hid the towels and snuck off the next day to buy new ones. Imagine if her mother found out she was pregnant before marriage and gave a baby up for adoption?

After finally opening the letter that evening, she quickly stuffed it in her suitcase and didn't call the caseworker who wrote it until she was home in Illinois.

"When I gave the baby up for adoption, I placed her in God's hands. No one except my husband has any idea about the pregnancy, and I want to keep it that way."

"I understand your hesitance, but I spoke with Ann myself. She sounds lovely."

"Ann?"

"Yes. That's what the adoptive parents named her."

"That's my mother's name."

"We find these coincidences often happen in adoptions and like to believe they are signs the unions are meant to be."

"That's all very nice, but I ask that you please not try to contact me again," she said before hanging up.

It was almost a year before I heard any news from the agency. And the conversation the caseworker relayed to me, my birth mother rejecting me for the second time, would serve as my only measure of the person she was for the next twenty years. Except this slight felt more personal than the first.

Diane confessed her secret to the man she married but never imagined he would use it as a weapon against her years later. Never tell a soul, especially a husband, if you want your past to remain there, and not come back to haunt you.

Diane's mother raised her and her siblings in the church, but the strict rules imposed upon the congregation seemed overly cautious until the unwanted pregnancy. Living in an apartment and hiding the baby bump from co-workers with only God by her side left her forever indebted to him. She worshiped the Bible in hopes that the rest of her life could be somehow less troublesome and raised her other children, who came along later accordingly, never exposing them to immorality.

Her husband also dedicated his life to the word of the Lord, but like many good Christians in private, he was something else entirely. After thirty-eight years of marriage, Diane left her abusive situation, packing up her car under the guise of needing to drop off a few things at the Goodwill, never to return.

It took him a minute to realize what happened and when he did, he used the skeleton in her closet like ammunition against her, telling her mother and the children what she had done so many years before. My siblings, in shock, begged her to search for me, and she agreed, except it was too late. Cinderella was born into a castle, already married her prince, had two children of her own, and no longer needed saving.

Don't get me wrong. I longed to meet my birth mother every single day for twenty years. I may have even lived my adult life as if I would meet her eventually, in a way that would make any mom proud.

Diane and I thrived in each other's company for three years, making anyone in our lives slightly envious of our perfect relationship. I considered it a miracle that we ever met and assured her it was perfect timing. My parents were deceased, so I didn't have to worry about hurting their feelings. And that's the part that doesn't sit well for me as an adoptee. Should I feel guilty for wanting to explore my background? Apps that break down your ethnicity were not around yet when I began to search, but beyond that, I wanted to know the story surrounding my birth, not only my heritage.

After not speaking to my birth father, Ben, for over forty years, Diane proudly presented me to him at his mother's house in Boynton Beach three months before he passed away from colon cancer.

It was eerie to stand in the hundred-year-old house where my birth parents met at a party in 1965 while his parents were away in Atlantic City. Little did they know that while they gambled their son, Ben, would offer Diane scotch, a girl who never tasted alcohol, they would start dating, and she would later become pregnant.

Ben's mother wanted them to marry and offered a place to live until they got on their feet, but it didn't solve the real problem. Diane's mother would still know her daughter had sex before marriage.

While I enjoyed the spotlight, meeting a slew of long-lost relatives from both sides, I didn't realize that Diane's reputation was still at stake. Whenever we told our story, I could feel her cringe, still afraid of how others would judge her.

After the reunion, Diane bought a condo in Florida and moved from Colorado to be closer to me. It was the first time she had lived alone and found comfort as always in a nearby church.

There she met a man named Joseph, who also had a past but tried to appear flawless and pure as she did. And before long, they had woven themselves into each other's lives, becoming the epitome of co-dependent and using Bible verses to talk their way in and out of any questionable behavior.

When she introduced all of us to him, no one thought they should marry.

"What's the purpose of getting married at this point?" I asked.

"God spoke to me and told me I should marry him," she said. And who would argue with that?

I attended the wedding in Indiana, but my relationship with Diane figuratively ended that day on the altar, between hymns. And I can't blame Joseph for it, although he was a creeper, using the excuse of being a self-proclaimed healer to touch other women.

My son, now the drum captain of the marching band in high school, had a performance one evening, and I toyed with whether or not to invite my mother and her new husband. I tolerated their strange churchy behavior, but my children didn't grow up around extreme religion, and it didn't help that Angelo called him Jim Jones at home, in private. I warned my family they might show up and only asked that they be polite.

As we all stood together, the drumline played accompanied by the color guard using flags for visual effect. We were all enjoying the show. Before I could stop her, my daughter, Teran, complained her back was bothering her, and Joseph asked if he could pray for her.

"Okay," she said, imagining the meeting with God would happen later in private, but Joseph placed his hand on her back and began praying for her healing, my mother following his lead with head bowed and eyes closed.

It felt like grace before dinner. Then too, we appeased them, although they never gave us a choice, grabbing our hands and droning on while the food got cold.

Diane is their biological grandmother, but my children grew up without her as I did, so it was easy for them to walk away. I was in the middle between my family and the version of my birth mother who I didn't recognize anymore since she met Joseph.

She asked me not to mention to anyone else about the adoption for fear I would tarnish her image to her new church friends and embarrass her husband, and she no longer spent time with me alone. The Creeper was always by her side for protection.

In the end, I thanked her for meeting me and giving me three years with her but backed out graciously, preserving the memories we made because whatever was happening in her life, we didn't want any part.

Angelo was the executive lieutenant at the time in Lauderdale by the Sea. Diane and Joseph lived in an apartment on the beach and were involved in a Bible study group with the most unsavory characters. Several incidences in their building required police assistance to solve, and when we tried to intervene, telling Diane that these people had criminal histories, she bucked back, defending their honor.

Finally, my half-brother, Kirk, got involved, and I passed them off to live closer to him. It was a relief to have them out of our hair, like misbehaved teens, and Diane and I didn't speak for years following the move.

So before calling her back, I remind myself of that painful time and try not to get sucked into her web.

"Ann! It's so good to hear your voice! I've been worried. The hospitals in Florida are so crowded."

"It's terrible here. The businesses closed for a while to get a handle on the number of cases."

"What about Angelo?"

"He's working a lot as usual, so I started writing. I think I've got enough for a book."

"I know you can do it if you want to. You always amaze me with your talent."

"Thanks, Mom."

"We have been attending church services virtually on Sunday mornings, and Joseph is doing all the shopping for me. I haven't felt well lately. I lay on the couch all day."

"Sorry to hear that. What's the matter?"

"Whenever I eat, I get pain in my stomach. I've had it before. I think it's reflux."

"I hope you feel better soon. I can send you a few chapters to entertain you while you lie there."

"I would love that."

I write in the mornings. And now, when I have to stop writing, my thoughts in mid-stream, to get ready for work, I wish I could return to my quarantine routine.

My witching hour was before dawn, when I didn't have to struggle to find words. I typed away for hours, but I could only write for so long, so I took a break to return phone calls at noon. My kids both checked in from home, where they now worked remotely.

I expected the dozens of calls from clients. When I told them we would be closed for two weeks, along with restaurants and fitness centers, they became anxious, habitually having their nails done for decades. But I couldn't believe my luck, two full weeks to write came at the perfect time, and writing kept me from the news and hourly reports of more deaths by the day.

When two weeks became eight, I was busy learning where a comma should go and past and present participle. My clients were desperate, the product still attached but dangling off the ends of their fingers like loose teeth. In one hour, I had two voicemails.

"My friend's nail tech is doing nails at home. Call me if you want me to drive over." I called her back and explained that my husband is on the Covid-19 task force at work and prefers I don't. Then another, "Would you be able to come to my house and do my nails while the salon is closed?" But I didn't falter. I had to keep writing if I was to finish the book before the salon reopened.

When I had nothing left to give my manuscript late afternoon, I changed into a pair of leggings and set out for a walk. I grabbed my phone to make notes of any epiphanies the exercise might spawn. Angelo and I had scheduled a Zoom happy hour with our friends that evening, and I was considering blow-drying my hair for the first time in a week.

As I rounded the intersection, listening to a book on my Audible app, a girl on rollerblades passed me and stopped. It was my neighbor Gina who I hardly recognized with her surgical mask. Why when she's outside? She comes toward me and then backs up in the grass until we are safely six feet apart.

"I had to get out of the house. My kids are all home from college and driving me crazy."

I laugh. It reminds me of when we all had babies at home.

"Where did you get the rollerblades?" I ask.

"I found them when I cleaned my garage the other day."

"I saw the mountain of discards on your driveway."

Gina wasn't the only one. We were all binge-watching Netflix shows on minimalism, creating a frenzy of letting go of what is no longer needed, keeping only the things that spark joy, and organizing said items within an inch of their lives.

"You look like you know what you're doing on those skates."

"I used to be pretty good. I'm just afraid to fall—no hospitals under any circumstances. I heard the nurses all have the virus but are still required to work because the facilities are short-staffed."

"That's scary." I feel the heaviness in my chest and read somewhere to know it's anxiety, give in to it, and then let it go. So I try.

An Amazon delivery truck passes us in the meantime.

"I hope my new grill is on that truck," Gina said. "I'm making chicken tonight for dinner."

With the possibility of eating in a restaurant or vacationing for the weekend taken away, we all had to invent ways to stay home and entertain ourselves. It didn't matter who you were or how much money you had. We were all in the same boat.

Unsure if every day would be our last, Angelo and I masked up and entered the stores once a week, searching for specialty items to prepare meals at home. The problem was that everyone was after the same products, and the warehouses and delivery trucks couldn't keep up. Even essential food items were in short supply, and the toilet paper aisle? Still empty.

Once we brought our food home, did we need to wipe it all down before putting it away? The news didn't offer comfort with varying opinions from the experts.

The bottom line was to stay home, where households went under the microscope. Now was not the time to be in an unhappy relationship or live in a studio apartment. To stay sane, we had to evolve. Angelo bought one of the last mountain bikes in the Bike Shop and got in the best shape of his life, and I continued writing short stories of gossip heard over the years in the salon.

Diane proofread for me, praising my work like any other proud mom. She even joined in writing her version of our story until we got to the uncomfortable part for her and vanished again. It's how some people cope.

We were back in the salon by May 28, wearing masks and gloves and a shield between every station when US Covid-19 deaths reached 100,000.

Even with precautions in place, many regular clients, too paralyzed by fear, didn't return after the quarantine lifted. This lull in bookings allowed a surge of new clients who we had never met before and would never recognize if we bumped into them outside the salon not wearing the mask. And we weren't sure how to proceed. One left me a frantic voice mail. "I'm sitting in the line for a Coronavirus test. Please call me back. I have a broken nail, and I would like to come in to have it fixed." Should I let her come in before she gets her results?

I was thankful for the case of latex gloves I purchased before the pandemic. They are one more layer of protection but doubled in price if you can even find them. Before, I only wore them to save my manicure and to save having to touch whatever was living under my client's artificial nails. I wash my hands till they are raw and wrinkled from all the soap and sanitizing gel I've been using and place a fresh pair on before removing Helen's polish one afternoon, revealing something dark underneath.

"It's probably chocolate. You'll clean that for me, right?" she asks.

I hand over the nail brush and point to the bathroom. Maybe after all these years, my patience is wearing thin, and then I check my phone. I have a text from Linda. She writes, *I'm sick. Can I still come in if I wear a mask?*

I haven't known Linda for that long. She's relatively new, and I can never hear what she says, her mumbles muffled by the mask, the blow dryers going, and our faces divided by the shield. I imagine her covering her mouth to cough or sneeze and then placing her hand in mine, as many clients do.

Let's reschedule for next week, I write. And realize I have become very much like the nail technicians in the walk-in salons, doing the nails of strangers.

CHAPTER THIRTEEN:

Alabama

I PREPARE TO BOARD MY EARLY MORNING FLIGHT bound for Alabama a year later, in 2021. I picture my birth mother, Diane, lying in a hospital bed, unable to swallow even a sip of water, and my throat constricts.

For months she suffered but held off seeing a doctor, afraid that when someone has had cancer, they will assume any new symptoms indicate another tumor. The last thing she wanted was endless blood tests and CAT scans only to hear bad news, but when the stomach aches became too painful to ignore and she could no longer will them away, Diane showed up in the emergency room with the Creeper by her side.

The doctors couldn't see the new tumor initially on the scans. I spoke to her after, and her spirits seemed lifted. Hope is all we ever need to feel instantly better, but the pain in her stomach eventually returned.

My half-brother Kirk happened to be visiting our mother for Thanksgiving. She'd tried to discourage him from coming, claiming she wasn't up to visitors, but he packed his new wife and baby into the car and hit the road anyway.

It was a comfortable ride from Utah to Mobile in the revenge car (the new Mercedes he purchased after the divorce from his first wife), stopping periodically along the way to accommodate the infant tucked carefully into the backseat. Meanwhile, Mom prepared for their arrival.

There is nothing like visitors to get you off the couch, no matter how sick you feel. Mom rallied, washing bedding and stocking the refrigerator, but Dina, Kirk's wife, had to take over the domestic responsibilities once they got there. Mom was in so much pain she ended up in the hospital before the turkey dinner made it to the table.

Thanksgiving marked the beginning of a three-month stay for the little family at Diane and Joseph's house. Every time they tried to leave, Mom would have another episode. Joseph couldn't care for himself, let alone our mother. Who knows what would have happened if not for Kirk's ability to work remotely.

Finally, early this morning, the doctors performed an exploratory surgery as a last alternative and found that cancer had spread throughout her abdomen.

When Kirk calls to tell me the news, I am with a client. I stop filing mid-nail to step outside so I can hear.

"There is nothing more they can do for Mom in the hospital. We are bringing her home. You better get on a plane if you want to see her," Kirk says.

"How long do we have?"

"She can't eat. So however long a person can live without food."

"Let me reserve a flight, and I will call you back."

As soon as I hang up, I dial Angelo's number.

"Can you find a flight for me to see my mom, leaving as soon as possible?"

"What about the virus? The hospital probably won't even let you in."

"They are sending her home."

"You want to stay in a house with those people?"

"Kirk will be there, and I have to go. I don't want to regret it later."

I hear the keys clicking on his computer through the phone.

"There is one flight out in the morning. When do you want to return?"

"I was thinking Wednesday."

"You're planning to be there for your birthday?"

"It's the last one I will spend with her."

During the flight, I pray our visit together will somehow be a fond memory, not another to add to my collection of painful ones. And if Diane's frame of mind during the long phone conversations we have had over the past few months is any indication, her emotional state is stable. I've seen her behavior when it was combative and vowed never to witness it again. She has never shown that side of herself to Kirk, and I am comforted by that.

Once the plane lands, I receive a text message from Christie, my youngest half-sibling, who arrived this morning from Montana. She has decided not to stay with us in the house and instead booked a room at a hotel.

I wanted to prepare you
Mom is not doing well
Her skin looks yellow

The thought of seeing her this way makes me feel weak. I wait at the curb for Kirk to pick me up in the bright sunshine on the clear fifty-degree day. I have seen death before, and know I can be a shoulder to lean on for my half-brother and two half-sisters. This visit with our mom is only the fourth time the four siblings will be together in one place, and it will be the last. Mom has always been the glue.

Finally, I spot Kirk's Mercedes heading toward me.

"Can you cook dinner tonight?" he asks once we are on the road.

"Sure."

"I was thinking about your picadillo. Dina has been doing all the cooking and cleaning since we got here for Thanksgiving, and she's exhausted."

"I'm sure. Between Mom and Christian."

"Yes. And he's teething, so it's been rough."

The car veers off the highway onto a ramp that takes us to the main road through town. I see a grocery store up ahead. Once I reach the house, I know I won't want to leave, so I suggest we stop now, and Kirk pulls into the parking lot.

Flattered that Kirk remembers the dish I once made him, I grab enough ingredients for a double recipe. My anxiety level is high, but the overhead music in the store is calming, so I continue to shop. I have no idea what my mom has in her house. I peruse the aisle with the specialty coffees, adding a few bottles of cold brew to my cart, then turn my attention to the red wine. Surprisingly this quiet town has a great selection. The wine will hopefully take the edge off of the difficult days ahead.

My new sister-in-law shows me to the sun-lit primary bedroom, where my mother lies trapped in a rented hospital bed, unable to move or even sit straight up. Diane looks beautiful in a blue cotton floral nightgown, smiling. Her smooth ivory complexion has none of the yellow tinges my sister mentioned. We hug for the first time in almost a year.

"My drains started working," Mom says to explain how well she seemed compared to the day before. She could at least swallow small sips of water without anything coming back up.

Just then, my phone rings—my husband's picture in his police uniform light up the screen.

"Are you there yet?"

"We just walked in."

"How is your mom?"

"She looks fine. I think she was only faking, so we would come and see her."

Mom laughs, and I get off the phone, promising to call back later.

"Mom, you do look great," I say.

"I feel so much better since I can drink a little water, and I thought I might try a little ice cream or some sherbet. Is it bad for me to have sugar?"

"I think it's okay. You probably don't have to worry about what you eat anymore."

I take my cues from her. Her ability to speak openly about her situation, even with a sense of humor, makes things easier. It is futile to avoid the subject or pretend she will recover.

"I think the doctor would say you can have anything that sounds good to you right now." I knew this to be true. What possible consequences could happen from a bit of sugar now?

"I wish we knew you wanted sherbet," I say. "Kirk and I just stopped at the store; we could have gotten it for you."

"Christie is picking up Melanie and Ruth from the airport later. They can get some for me. Maybe the orange kind?" Melanie is my other half-sister, and Ruth is her eight-year-old daughter. They are flying in from Colorado.

My birth mother moved around her entire life. And in the ten years since she met Joseph, they lived in eight different residences. This house they bought sight unseen on the internet. The crown molding, wallpaper, and other high-end finishes made it a showpiece in the Nineties. Now it seems slightly worn and dated yet still charming.

"I'm so glad we bought such a big house. It's the perfect size for all of you to stay here together," Mom says. And I wonder what she thinks of Christie staying in a hotel.

"Not many people get to attend their funeral," she continues.

She has a point. Better for us to be with her now. If she were here lying in her casket, we would have missed the chance to say our last goodbyes.

"And I don't want a traditional funeral. My neighbor just died, and the funeral home posted his obituary on their website, where friends and family can comment and share pictures. I want everyone to go to their website to honor me."

"Okay," I say, rapidly processing the words coming at me, more manic than depressive.

"And I called a realtor today to sell the house," she says, taking preplanned funeral arrangements to the next level. She had a virtual checklist to complete before closing her eyes for the last time.

"They want to list it next week."

"Where will Joseph go?"

"He wants to live in Indiana near his son."

The son is also churchy but amazingly normal compared to his father.

Next to the hospital bed is an upholstered chair.

"This is the significant person chair," Mom says. "Everyone has been taking turns sitting in it. Go ahead, Ann."

I go to my bag and then sit, handing her several photos of the two of us together. Slowly, she looks at them, smiling. We both looked so happy when we met in 2007, and the joy of reconnecting carried us through for a time.

We have been speaking again lately, and I asked her before I left if there was anything I could bring her from Florida. Nail polish was the only thing she wanted, so I showed her the creamy coral pink shade I chose.

"I love this color," she says.

Last manicures are a gift I have given to many clients and loved ones. Sending them out of this world with fresh polish makes me feel like I help prepare them in some small way.

I notice how attractive her hands and feet still are, and I consider it a waste that she's not old and decrepit. At seventy-six years old, her skin is still peaches and cream. It's hard to fathom she will be gone in mere days or weeks.

Of course, only God knows when we will take our last breath, but after the manicure, I type how long a person can live without food into my phone and Google the answer anyway. I imagine my siblings have done the same. I get various answers, but without food, not long is the average consensus. At this moment, though, she still seems to have a ton of energy.

"Can you help me pack up my closet? I need you to do it. I hate the thought of strangers going through my things. There are some boxes in the next room where Joseph is staying. You girls will sleep here with me."

I feel safe in this room with her, and knowing I won't have to be alone with Joseph wandering around is a relief. I make my way down the hall to a room with a single bed and see the boxes stacked up.

I thought it would be easy to fold what she has and pack the items away, but she wants to participate.

"That one is new; maybe you want to keep it?" she asks as I hold up a frilly tank top. I put it aside with no intention of taking it. Seeing it after she's gone would be too emotional, and I move on to the long-sleeved tops.

"Aww, that one I got in the gift shop on one of our trips to Bermuda. It's too big for you, but it would look good on Melanie. Put it aside for her," she says. And I put it aside. The girls walk in from the airport, and Christie seems repulsed by what I'm doing. "How can you do this while she is still alive?"

"She asked me to," I say, not offended.

If not for Christie, I would not be standing in this room next to my mother's deathbed because Diane would never have looked for me on her own. Like many birth mothers, forgetting it ever happened is the only way to cope with the decision to give up a child. Christie is the one who begged her to find me after a miscarriage she suffered.

Religion always brought my mother comfort, so she dove into it after relinquishing her rights to me and let it swallow her whole. She and her first husband attended services, worked in the church, and raised their three children by the strict rules demanded of the Christian life. They didn't drink, dance, watch television, or let their daughters play with Barbies. It was much the same as the way her mother raised her.

I couldn't be more opposite from my siblings if I tried, and standing with them in this bedroom feels like a competition: the children she raised against the new sparkly one. New is always more exciting, but I try to blend in. My siblings, who grew up with our mother, have resentments from childhood. Thankfully, we avoided all that.

Mom falls asleep, so I let her rest and join the others in the kitchen to prepare dinner. Seeing she's in no imminent danger allows my appetite to return, and suddenly I need to eat.

The house is ranch-style with a wraparound porch. I walk through the living room with wallpaper and matching curtains reaching the high ceilings to the kitchen. French doors lead out to the backyard from every direction, and brown leaves cover the ground under tall bare trees.

Kirk's second wife, Dina, holds the baby in her arms and watches as I chop onions and peppers on the long kitchen island. Ironically, I look the most like Diane of all her children, and Christian has our dark features.

"I can't believe you guys have been here since Thanksgiving," I say.

"I can't either," Dina says in her heavy Italian accent.

"What is it? Three months already?"

"We couldn't leave her alone with Joseph."

"Good idea."

"We even packed our things last week to go, but then we had to take Mom back to the hospital."

Joseph walks into the kitchen, and it dawns on me that I never have to speak to this man again after this trip, and I smile to myself.

He was tall and handsome for his age and still had a full head of hair when my mother met him. The other ladies in bible study flirted with him, but he worked his way over to my mother and asked for her phone number. At first, she said no. Her thirty-eight-year marriage ended in a contentious divorce, which she hadn't yet recovered.

"We can be friends," he said to her in his soft, creepy voice.

He called the same night. Years of pain and resentment melted her heart as he spoke, and a door cracked open there, filtering light like the sun shining after a winter of clouds. A warmth came over her, familiar from long ago, before the unwanted pregnancy and the unhappy marriage, and it felt like hope. Diane grabbed onto the feeling and refused to let go.

I was the first to meet Joseph and watched how his God-talk made my mother melt. If there were a cliff around, she would have followed him off of it.

Joseph took tons of supplements, exercised daily, and believed he was immortal, or at the very least, he would live to a hundred and thirty. We saw this as a red flag, but our reluctance to accept him made Mom angry with us. After they got engaged, we learned Joseph had four previous wives, but this news didn't discourage our mother.

She stopped having a glass of wine with dinner, and when I mentioned this to Christie, she said, "We thought it was odd when she drank. We had never seen her drink before she met you." And I wondered what else I didn't know.

It took me longer than it should have to pull away after finally finding the woman who gave birth to me. No one had ever started drama with me as a way to separate, but better to end on a high note than to slowly chip away at our relationship with more hurt feelings and misunderstandings. Parentless once again, it felt almost like a relief when it was over. Maybe withholding my love toward her was a payback. Maybe subconsciously, I wanted to abandon her the way she rejected me at birth and then again when I tried to find her.

It turns out Joseph is not immortal. He's aged tremendously since the last time I saw him. My mother mentioned there might be some dementia, but it seems part of his act. I flashback to how he would pull me into an inappropriate hug, and I ask how he is doing, keeping my distance.

"I'm doing okay," he says, looking slightly pathetic.

Joseph keeps Mom company while the rest of us eat. In the bedroom, she tries a few bites of the sherbet, and at first, it seems to taste good to her.

We eat like we are starving in the dining room, and I enjoy listening to my siblings' banter. After a few bites, I hear Kirk say, "Patty and I are sleeping in one of the rooms down the hall."

He meant to say Dina and not Patty, his ex-wife's name, but no one corrects him. Dina has slipped into Patty's spot so seamlessly.

After dinner, I pour myself a glass of wine in the corner and sip it whenever I pass by. It tastes so good in the antique cut crystal glasses that once belonged to Joseph's mother.

When I return to the bedroom, Mom is uncomfortable.

"I won't try that again," she says, pointing to the tiny sherbet cup.

And after that, there was only water. Lots of water, pitcher after pitcher. Then she asks for the bedpan.

Hospice doesn't send someone to do the dirty work. If you take a loved one home to live out the final days, you either hire a private nurse or care for them yourself. We didn't have a nurse.

Melanie pulls the covers back and slips on a pair of disposable gloves like a pro. She hands the pan to me, and I carry it to the bathroom to flush it down the toilet. Next, we clean her and pull a fresh adult-sized diaper over her hips. The irony was my mother never had to change my diapers, but here I was, changing hers. Sometimes we are reminded of the endless amount of strength we are born with and never need to access.

"Thank you, girls, for being here. Kirk and Patty have done so much and can finally relax."

Mom did it, too. The habit of saying Kirkandpatty for over thirty years like it was one word, like they were one person was hard to break. I wondered how many times Dina caught them calling her Patty. And what would Patty think? I'm sure she never imagined the husband she threw away would find another so soon.

That night I am woken from my sleep.

"Water. I need ice water," Mom says. I jump up, hand her the glass, and wait for her to drink.

"I will get more ice," Melanie says, and I go with her to the kitchen.

Dina is standing there with the baby, and we whisper to each other for a few minutes. Then, we hear our phones vibrate through the walls. Mom is texting us. My message says,

Ann, do you have your phone with you?
I feel lonely.

We laugh in the dark, careful not to wake the others. Mom pressures herself to keep her eyes open so she won't "miss the party." When she finally drifts off, her cough wakes her.

"When I fall asleep, I feel like I'm choking," she says. She is on a low dose of morphine and an anti-anxiety medication.

We get up again to empty the drains hanging from her sides during the night. I hold my breath. The fluid reminds me of a vacuum cleaner we used to have where dust mixes with water in the tank and comes out like mud.

In the morning, Mom and I are the only ones awake. I sit in the significant person's chair as the sun shines through the blinds.

"I feel bad leaving you," she says.

"We have lived in separate places before," I say, thinking about the years I survived without her.

"Kirk will miss me terribly, but he will be fine as long as he has you."

"If someone remembers us, we are still here."

"True." Mom looks down at her phone. "What do you think I should do with my iPhone? It's brand new."

"Mom, you never have to worry about that stuff again."

"I guess you're right."

She has me go into a drawer where she has every card I ever sent her. Most I bought blank and wrote a verse inside since it is impossible to find a card appropriate for our situation. 'You have always been there for me' didn't exactly fit.

The nurse calls and ups the dose of morphine and an anti-anxiety medication we give her at night. We walk the neighborhood while mom rests, and I suggest a sibling photo.

"No, I didn't dress for a picture," Melanie says.

"Okay, later."

Christie gets in Melanie's face with a sugary voice. "Mel, it's okay if you don't want to take a picture; we don't have to do it now. Don't feel bad if you want to say no. It's okay."

"I don't need your permission to take a picture or not take a picture," Melanie snaps.

I recognized the outburst. It wasn't what was said as much as how it was delivered. Mom's words stung me many times the same way. I never understood using words as weapons. Christie seems unfazed, though probably used to it, and walks ahead of us with Ruth.

I stay back with Melanie, who is back to speaking softly. "I don't know why I talk to her like that. I don't feel that way toward her."

Before bed, I fill the water pitcher on the second evening, so we don't have to do it during the night. As I carry it back to the room, I hear Mom say to Joseph, "You are why my cancer came back." Kind of harsh, but I'm sure she has her reasons.

As we start to fall asleep that night, a thunderstorm begins outside. We hear the rain coming down hard against the windows.

"Isn't it a nice rainstorm? I love the rain," Mom says.

Once I realize the heavier dose of drugs makes her talk in her sleep, and I don't need to participate in the conversation, I stay quiet. Finally, she is calm.

Mom and I wake up on the morning of my birthday before the sun rises. I slip out of bed without disturbing Melanie and Ruth and into the "significant person" chair.

Mom reaches under her blanket and hands me a birthday card in a pink envelope.

"I wanted to be the first to wish you a happy birthday." It's sweet. She is on her deathbed, still wanting to make a memory for me.

"I could hear you last night in the dining room during dinner," she says.

"We were having a great time."

"I imagine when I am in heaven, I will hear your laugh," she says.

Then she starts to cry. I wonder how I can again reassure her she did the right thing by giving me away so many years ago when she was a mere child. I will never forget her bravery. The words I want to say are still floating around in my head when it becomes clear I'm not the reason she's crying.

"My hairdresser is coming to pick up the dogs today."

"Oh?"

"Joseph is not a dog person. Once I'm gone, no one will take care of them. I can't believe they are leaving the same day I lost you, fifty-five years ago," she sobs.

I barely even noticed the two fat Bichons, if not for their toenails tapping incessantly on the hardwood floors.

"I was okay, and they will be, too," is all I can muster.

I think she might rest, but another task needs doing.

"Can you take out my jewelry? I want everyone to pick something to remember me."

I find several velvet boxes in a drawer, and I leave her to sort through them and answer my birthday text messages from my kids and a few friends. When Mom falls back to sleep, I take my shower and eat breakfast. When I come back to the room, my phone is blowing up.

There are several missed calls from Angelo, and the phone rings again.

"Where were you? I tried calling you and texting you."

"Angelo, it's only eight thirty here."

"I didn't speak to you last night or this morning. I was about to send the police. I thought that Joseph killed you all in your sleep."

"If you saw him now, you wouldn't worry. I could fight him."

"I tried to call your brother, and he doesn't answer either."

"I went to sleep early, and you know Kirk never has his phone."

"Okay. I will speak to you later."

It is typical for Angelo to worry. I should be more diligent about calling, but time seems to stand still in the house where my mother lies dying.

Kirk adds candles to a cake Dina's mom sent from Italy. It tastes like sweet bread covered in powdered sugar, light and airy. While mom sleeps, we have lunch and everyone, including Kirk's older boys who have just arrived, sings to me in the formal dining room. Then Ruth, an exceptional child, performs a song on the violin. She is a prodigy as my son is on the drums. My fifty-fifth birthday is the first with my siblings and the most memorable ever.

We are all in the kitchen cleaning up from lunch when Kirk says, "I heard you in here earlier. I was thinking, how did Mom make it to the kitchen? You sounded just like her." I smile. I am another version of her to him, and I plan to be there for him emotionally after she's gone.

I walk across the house to check on Mom. Ruth has the jewelry sprawled across the king-sized bedspread, eyes wide in amazement. But Melanie is upset.

"I don't want Ruth to think taking your jewelry is okay! We care about you, not your things." I am tearing up listening to Melanie's outpouring of emotion. Her mother is dying before her, and I don't know how much more intensity I can take. Mom stays calm, though.

"I thought you would have something to remember me. If you don't take it, it will all go to Goodwill," she says in a sweet voice. I could tell she was determined not to get ruffled.

Melanie and Christie also had their issues with Mom. I was never privy to what they were exactly. When they surface, no one explains them to me. I wonder how I may have fared in this family had I grown up with them.

The last evening, we get pizza delivered, and Mom is in the bedroom with Joseph.

"I told Mom she should give Joseph permission to remarry," Kirk says.

"That's what she is doing?" I ask. "I didn't know that was a thing."

"Ya. It's the right thing to do."

Kirk probably would not have been so concerned with Joseph's feelings had he known at the time that all of his inheritance would belong to Joseph in the end. Their will states that the spouse left behind receives any marital property. Mom is Joseph's third wife to die and leave him all their money.

In the morning, I wake early and dress for the trip home. I never unpacked my bag, so I zip it back up and carry it to the front door. Kirk waits in the car to drive me to the airport. And then the vomiting starts.

I never got used to my role as a caregiver in this situation, and I didn't escape the final obstacle. The vomit seeps under my mother onto the sheet between her and the plastic mattress. Her beautiful nightgown is saturated.

"Can you help me bathe her before you go?" Melanie asks.

"Yes," I say, and my heart begins to pound as I hold a small garbage can to my mother's mouth. I would do anything for Melanie. She accepted me as her sister wholeheartedly even including me as a bridesmaid in her wedding after knowing me only a short time.

She walks toward me with a gold-colored hard plastic pan of warm water and hands me a pair of disposable gloves. I line up several damp washcloths doused in waterless body wash that hospice sent over. Mom winces in pain as we undress her, and I clean the surgical wound while Melanie wipes the rest of her.

The long incision stretching the length of her stomach from the surgery is now red and inflamed. It is impossible to move her off the bed because she's in pain, but rolling her from side to side, we dress her in a clean nightgown and place a fresh sheet underneath her.

"When I get to heaven, I will thank your parents for taking care of you," she says before I go.

From that point on, Mom requires tedious care. The surgical wound needs new dressings every hour, even during the night.

The following day, Mom still sounded like herself, just slightly weaker.

"Joseph will have my phone after I'm gone," she says. "He will probably call all of you because he will have my contacts. Don't answer him; he's evil." And I wonder why she didn't leave whatever she had to my siblings if he's so bad. Then she says, "My life would have never been complete if I never met you."

"Mine either," I tell her. And I mean it.

My parents knew nothing about my birth family. In those years, where a baby came from didn't matter to a couple who desperately wanted a child, and they assumed how they raised me determined the adult I would become. No one gave much thought to the part heredity played.

I can go for the next forty years without speaking to Diane. I've done it before. Even with all the pain that came with our relationship, I'm content with my decision to meet her. Meeting someone who looks like me, willing to answer all my questions was closure I never expected to find.

When Mom can no longer speak, Kirk and I agree that he will send me a text when she takes her last breath, and I can call him when I am ready. I'm home from work only minutes the following Friday when he sends the message.

We think she has passed.

Can't feel a pulse.

Calling hospice.

I'm not crying. I wait a few minutes and then call.

"We are waiting for the funeral home to come and pick her up. Melanie and Dina are doing her hair," Kirk says.

"Aww, she would have loved that."

"I will always cherish my memories of Mom," he says.

"You have many more memories than I have."

"Those years were not as good. Our father was pretty abusive."

Again I am reminded of my parents, who adopted me and unselfishly raised me as their own.

Before bed, my phone rings, and Diane's name and photo appear on the caller ID. Seeing her appear as before on the screen is unsettling, but then I think it might be Kirk calling from her phone, so I answer it, but it's Joseph.

"Hi, Ann."

"Hi Joseph, I'm sorry for your loss."

"I just called to tell you that your mother loved you so much. She talked about you all the time. She was such a beautiful person."

"She was."

"She died at five forty. Her nails sure looked beautiful."

Not sure what to say, I hang up without saying goodbye, block the number from my phone, and get under the covers.

Finally, tears drip from my eyes, not just for Diane but for all the people I have lost in my lifetime. And for the baby I once was, abandoned at birth, tossed into the world, then blessed by so many.

After a few days off to honor my mother, I will return to the salon more aware of the conversations around me. Instead of talking about my trip to Alabama, I will encourage my clients to share what is happening in their lives, and I will do what I do best. I will listen.

"You must learn from the mistakes of others because you can't live long enough to make them all yourself."
Unknown